Dear Bear

by Joanna Harrison

Carolrhoda Books, Inc./Minneapolis

For James,
Katie
and Hugo.
xxx

With special thanks to my daughter Katie, aged six, for
writing and illustrating Katie's letters to the bear.

This edition first published in 1994 by Carolrhoda Books, Inc.

This book is available in two editions:
Library binding by Carolrhoda Books, Inc.
Soft cover by First Avenue Editions
c/o The Lerner Group
241 First Avenue North
Minneapolis, Minnesota 55401

LIBRARY OF CONGRESS CATALOGING-IN-PUBLICATION DATA

Harrison, Joanna
    Dear Bear / by Joanna Harrison.
        p. cm.
    Summary: Katie is afraid of the bear that lives under the stairs in her house,
until they exchange letters and she finally gets to meet him.
    ISBN 0-87614-839-9
    ISBN 0-87614-965-4 (pbk.)
    [I. Teddy Bears—Fiction. 2. Letters—Fiction. 3. Fear—Fiction.] 1. Title
PZ7.H252De 1994
[E]—dc20
                                                    93-44730
                                                        CIP
                                                        AC

Printed and bound in Thailand

7 8 9 10 11 - OS - 08 07 06 05 04

Katie liked having tea parties. It meant she didn't have to think about the bear.

Well, the bear didn't worry her that much. After all, it didn't bother her when she was busy at home…

...and she could even laugh about it at school.

But when she was at home in bed, however hard she tried, she couldn't stop thinking about the bear who lived under the stairs. She had never seen him, but she knew he was there, just waiting to jump out and grab her.

Sometimes huge bear-like shadows would chase her up the stairs. Katie decided to tell her parents about it.

She tried her dad, but he was
too busy vacuuming.

Her mom said, "Why don't you write the bear a letter and
tell him to go away?"

So Katie took out her pencils and paper and wrote the bear a letter.

She put it in an envelope

and left it outside the closet door.

This is what it said:

The next morning, the letter was gone. In its place was another one. It was addressed to Katie. It read:

UNDER THE STAIRS

DEAR KATIE,
I HAVE
TAKEN YOUR ADVICE
AND GONE AWAY.
I AM MUCH IN NEED
OF A VACATION FROM
SITTING IN THE CLOSET
ALL DAY
LOVE FROM
BEAR xx

P.S. BACK MONDAY.

During the next few days

Katie couldn't stop thinking...

...about the bear

on vacation.

But when Monday came, Katie didn't want to come home from school.

When she arrived home, she found a package in front of the closet door. Katie opened it up.

Inside was a little glass dome filled with snow.

With it was this card:

DEAR KATIE,
JUST A LITTLE
PRESENT I BOUGHT
FOR YOU WHILE
I WAS ON VACATION
LOVE FROM
BEAR XX
P.S. IT'S NICE TO BE BACK.

Katie showed her dad. "How
generous," he said. "Why don't you
write him a thank you letter?"

After Katie had written her letter, she put it in an envelope and dropped it over the banister.

It read:

Dear Bear Thankyou for my present. love from Katie x
Here it is on my piano

There was no reply the next day...

or the day after...

or the day after that.

Katie started to worry about the bear, so she wrote him another letter. This is what it said:

The next day, she received this reply:

Katie rushed to show her mom.

Her mom was very concerned.

"We'll make him a hot-water bottle,

some sandwiches,

and a nice cup of tea."

Katie knocked on the closet door. "Dear Bear," she whispered, "are you all right?" There was no answer.

The next morning the tray was gone. In its place was a letter.

Katie read the letter to her parents. "I see the Bears won again," said her father. He wasn't really listening.

Katie spent all the next afternoon getting ready

for her tea party with the bear. She put on her best outfit and

even brushed her hair.

But when four o'clock came, she wasn't so sure she wanted to go. After all, he was still the bear in the closet.

"Go on," said her mom, "he'll be expecting you."

And…

...he was.

For Smith...the bello who makes everything I create the most bella.

San Casciano
(Toscana)

LA
INSPIRATION AND RECIPES FROM THE

BELLA
CREATOR OF BELLA CUCINA ARTFUL FOOD

VITA

ALISA BARRY

Photography Rob Brinson

BELLA CUCINA ARTFUL FOOD
MEDITERRANEAN-INSPIRED FOODS
MADE IN THE U.S.A.

www.bellacucina.com

ART DIRECTION: Smith Hanes
PHOTOGRAPHY: copyright ©2003 by Rob Brinson
DUST COVER DESIGN: Louise Fili
DESIGN: Katja Burkett and Pamela Zuccker

Published by Bella Cucina Artful Food
Printed in the United States

FIRST EDITION
10 9 8 7 6 5 4 3 2

LA BELLA VITA

Inspiration & Recipes from the Creator of
Bella Cucina Artful Food

Photographed on location in San Casciano dei Bagni, Tuscany, Italy

AL MERCATO
TO THE MARKET

When the crisp morning air meets the
awakening day, the market streets are bustling.
Clusters of men gather in the piazza for their
morning espresso and animated talk
of politics, people, and what
la donna might be preparing for the
afternoon pranzo lunch.

{ TO BE A PART OF THIS DAILY RITUAL IS
TO BE A PART OF A CENTURIES-OLD ART OF LIVING
A BEAUTIFUL LIFE. }

I can only imagine their delicious
fate as I see the women scurry down to the market
with colorful bags, anxious to fill them with the
day's offerings. A glimpse of crusty
bread and fluffy fennel tops stirs thoughts
of Finocchio alla Griglia~fresh fennel
roasted on a wood-fired grill.

A DELICIOUS APPRECIATION
BETWEEN TWO CULTURES AND THE POSSIBILITIES
IN BETWEEN.

FOREWORD

CONTRIBUTED *by* JOANNE WEIR

*A*s a cookbook author, television host, and cooking teacher, I have been fortunate enough to meet many, many talented students and colleagues throughout my career. However, Alisa Barry stands out for me! It has been years since we first met in San Francisco. Alisa was my student and still I recall our first meeting. What was it that caught my attention that day? Was it her broad smile? Her contagious energy? Her charisma and charm? Or was it her unparalleled style? It was all of those things and more.

I remember a few months after we first met; I asked her to go to the San Francisco Farmer's Market and then invited her back to my house to cook lunch together. I thought I had a lot of energy and enthusiasm, but when the two of us were together, we were unstoppable. We had a billion ideas and wanted to cook everything! We filled our baskets with produce of all colors and shapes: heirloom tomatoes, rose garlic, sweet tender basil, just-picked white corn, Romano beans, and baby salad greens. For the rest of the afternoon, we cooked and talked. We opened a chilled bottle of Bandol rosé, sat on my city balcony amid the flowers and cityscape views, and ate chilled tomato soup and summer vegetable risotto.

This is what I call LA BELLA VITA, the beautiful life! We enjoyed it that day, and you can enjoy it wherever you may live.

LA BELLA VITA IS TAKING TIME TO SHOP FOR
THE FRESHEST SEASONAL FRUITS AND VEGETABLES
AT YOUR FAVORITE FARMER'S MARKET OR,
BETTER YET, PICKING THEM FROM YOUR OWN GARDEN.

It's cooking with friends and family, pouring a glass of good wine, and spending time at the table eating, talking, and sharing stories, recipes, and just the everyday routines of life. This is what Alisa and I shared that day but continue to enjoy. This is what life is about!

Alisa Barry at Chiusi Market in Tuscany, Italy

As my parents often remind me as they recount stories from my childhood, my love of food began long before it was to become my life's work. They recall memories of me, at the tender age of six, standing on a chair, stirring vigorously at the stovetop. I was already lost in the pleasures of cooking. Weekends were spent on our farm in Wisconsin, where we were encouraged to experience whatever was at hand. We were exposed to things that I later learned would greatly influence my education and my appreciation for solitude, simplicity, and fresh, seasonal foods.

Memories of freshly harvested morels after a
rainy spring day, dipped in a light egg and flour batter
and sautéed in sizzling sweet cream butter.
Never since have I tasted morels
so sweet and earthy, so moist and delicious.

And the raspberries, plump and perfect with a fragrance and flavor that can only be found in fresh-picked fruit. As I lay in bed contemplating getting up, my mom would head out to harvest the berries, still wet with morning dew. Hot oatmeal slathered in brown sugar and christened with this lovely garnish was her favorite.

I remember the riches from the overgrown, untended garden... oozing rivers of Concord grape juice staining my hands and mouth as I spit out the seeds and chew on the tough-textured skins. I can still taste the rhubarb, tart and sour, not waiting for the promise of a delicious oven-baked crisp or flaky-crusted pie. These were our snacks. No doubt I longed for junk food, as most kids do, and tried to sneak candy wherever I could, but somehow the adventure of the experience in the country was fascinating for this city kid.

Later in my childhood, we moved to a house with more land, which allowed my father to create an organic garden. At the time, the butter-laden rutabaga and Brussels sprouts seemed a cruel punishment to my six brothers and sisters and me, and we laughed at my dad as he smiled with each bite. Now I know how wise this man was. My appreciation for his commitment to his own passion grows with every year as I, too, come to appreciate what really matters in life.

And there were other treasures, now just a memory, that have contributed not only to my love of cooking, but also to my passion for eating deliciously well.

I still remember so vividly to this day being with my family in Mexico and reveling in the scent and beauty of watching freshly shucked, tender oysters sizzling over a hardwood fire on the beach.

I sat in envy, watching the locals prepare them for the people next to us on the beach that day. I didn't even know if I liked oysters, but the ritual and the freshness of this delicacy intrigued me.

During my college years, I ventured off to experience life in Europe. Living a year in Spain confirmed my passion for indulging in the foods and places that make life truly beautiful. My palate was changing and my appreciation for interesting foods was expanding. I knew at this moment where my future path was to take me. Upon my return to the states, I promptly began my research for cooking schools.

My culinary adventure was to continue and develop while cooking and living in Northern California. This magical and educational experience was to set the stage and solidify my lifelong philosophy of the art of food. I know how fortunate I am to have found my passion and to have had the opportunity to work with talented chefs, winemakers, and others as passionate as I about cooking and eating deliciously.

Living in Northern California, I developed a love of Mediterranean flavors. With a knowledgeable and enthusiastic guide, I began to travel to Italy and France to experience first-hand the treasures this land has to offer. I fell in love with Italy instantly—the people, the language, the food. My connection with this unpretentious and passionate place was immediate and long-lasting.

Today, I continue to travel to Italy several times yearly for inspiration and education. There I relish in the abundance of ingredients that are difficult to find at home in the Southeast. I spend most of my time in the Italian countryside at local markets and cooking in the kitchen, developing recipes with newly discovered ingredients and using traditional favorites.

In the end, I have learned that it is the meal, simply prepared and honest in its integrity of ingredients, preparation, and presentation that makes for a soulful food experience. And like you, I am often too busy to cook every meal. The key is to take time out to stop and savor, no matter how simple it may be. A glass of wine with a slice of crusty bread and round of creamy cheese, a caffé latte and biscotti in the afternoon. I am grateful almost every day for having had this and many other experiences throughout my life. I aspire daily to live authentically, soulfully, and simply. It is, indeed, a beautiful life—LA BELLA VITA!

Buon Appetito!
Alisa Barry

Simplicity

I HAVE FOUND THIS IS THE KEY TO ALL GREATNESS.
RESTRAINT IS A RARE GIFT. AND PASSION IS
A CHOICE, ALMOST A RESPONSIBILITY TO CHOOSE.
A WAY OF LIFE. A BEAUTIFUL LIFE.

A warm breeze brushes up
against my hair as I gingerly take
my first bite of

{ Zucchini Blossom
Risotto... }

Gentle, delicate, and short-lived,
like late summer nights, the blossoms
symbolize the seasonal bounty
we savor and celebrate.

Golden bursts of sweet,
sumptuous sun enliven my taste buds.
I remember why summer,
in its sensuous beauty, makes
me come alive.

❧

Table of Contents

Antipasti

{ Appetizers }

ARTISAN CHEESES WITH
LEMON PEAR MARMELLATA

OLIVE AND WARM FETA
CHEESE ANTIPASTI

SICILIAN CAPONATA EGGPLANT DIP

WHITE BEAN AND TOMATO BRUSCHETTA

CITRUS-MARINATED GRILLED SHRIMP
WITH PRESERVED ORANGE AIOLI

GRILLED SCALLOP SPIEDINI WITH
PRESERVED LEMON CREAM VINAIGRETTE

GRILLED FIGS WITH PROSCIUTTO
AND CHESTNUT HONEY

Artisan Cheeses with Lemon Pear Marmellata

*Raymond Hook, our local cheesemonger, has
brought many local and European artisan cheeses to our area.
We've held cheese tastings at Bella Cucina,
pairing them with our marmellatas as antipasti,
snacks, and desserts, to find out which cheeses best complement our
artisanally made condiments. Everyone at Bella Cucina
has a personal favorite, but we think the following
cheeses recommended by Raymond are the perfect
pairings with our marmellatas.*

*Lemon Pear Marmellata is especially delicious
with these cheeses because it has a tart yet subtly sweet,
complex combination of flavors.*

— Tomme —

An aged cow's milk cheese that tends to have a somewhat
soft texture and mellow flavor. You can find domestic, regionally
produced as well as imported varieties.

— French Pyrenees —

Our favorite is Abbaye de Belloc—an aged sheep's
milk cheese handmade by monks from their own herds at
their abbey in the Pyrenees Mountains.

— Majorero —

An aged goat's milk cheese from Spain. Typical
of Spanish flavors, this cheese is rubbed with paprika
for a slightly peppery, pungent taste.

— Robiola Due Latte —

Robiola is made by many producers. This particular
variety is a mixed cow's and sheep's milk cheese from northern
Italy. Its texture is very soft and creamy, almost rindless.

✦

Serving a carefully selected sampling of cheeses representing
a variety of tastes and textures will satisfy everyone's palate without
overwhelming them. Buy a small piece of a different type of cheese each
week to find out what tastes you like. If you are lucky enough to have
a cheesemonger in your neighborhood, ask for recommendations.

Serves 6

WITH THE WIDE VARIETY OF CHEESES AVAILABLE
TODAY AT YOUR SPECIALTY GROCER, LOCAL CHEESE SHOP,
OR EVEN GROCERY STORE, THE POSSIBILITY OF TRYING NEW AND
ENTICING VARIETIES OF CHEESE IS ENDLESS.

HAVE FUN EXPERIMENTING WITH TASTING
DIFFERENT FLAVORS.

❧

TAKING TIME TO COOK FOR FRIENDS AND
FAMILY IS A LUXURY I WOULD GLADLY SACRIFICE
ALL OTHER RICHES TO ENJOY.

The dry earth crackles beneath
my feet as the sun beats down upon the fruit.

The vines patiently
await the coolness of the eve.

And soon at harvest
we will drink.

OLIVE AND WARM FETA CHEESE ANTIPASTI

*You will be amazed at how these simple ingredients
are transformed when baked. The texture of the feta becomes
creamy and its flavor is enhanced by soaking up the
oils and herbs. The olives become meaty when warm and soft,
and because they have been infused with the flavors of lemon,
bay leaf, and garlic, they sing of the Mediterranean.*

---

6 ounces sheep's milk feta cheese

1 teaspoon fresh thyme leaves

¼ teaspoon freshly cracked black pepper

½ cup drained BELLA CUCINA Antipasti Olives
(plus 2 tablespoons reserved oil)

1 tablespoon BELLA CUCINA Sicilian Lemon Aromatic Oil

∞

PREHEAT OVEN TO 350°F.
Place the cheese in an ovenproof dish and top with the
thyme and pepper, pressing lightly so that they stick to the cheese.
Sprinkle the olives around the cheese and pour the
reserved oil over the cheese.

Bake 15 to 20 minutes, until cheese is golden on
top and brown on the bottom, bubbling around the edges.
Remove from oven. Transfer the cheese and the olives
to a serving platter and drizzle with the lemon oil.
Alternatively, serve the cheese directly from the baking dish for
a more rustic presentation *(this also keeps the cheese warm)*.

*Serve warm with crostini rounds or
Bella's Dipping Crackers.*

SERVES 6

SICILIAN CAPONATA EGGPLANT DIP

*Even those who don't particularly like eggplant fall in love with our
Roasted Eggplant Pesto. This recipe pairs our pesto with sweet and
tangy flavors for a variation on the traditional Sicilian dip.
It also makes a delicious sauce when heated and tossed with penne
pasta and freshly grated Parmigiano-Reggiano or as
a filling for baked stuffed eggplant.*

FOR THE RAISINS:

¼ cup Vin Santo ✺ 2 tablespoons golden raisins

❧

¼ cup BELLA CUCINA Extra Virgin Olive Oil

I cup diced eggplant

¼ cup diced yellow onion ✺ ¼ cup diced celery

One 6-ounce jar BELLA CUCINA Roasted Eggplant Pesto

I tablespoon BELLA CUCINA Sun-Dried Tomato Pesto

I tablespoon drained capers

2 tablespoons toasted pine nuts

I teaspoon chopped fresh garlic

I tablespoon chopped Italian flat-leaf parsley

I teaspoon red wine vinegar

Kosher salt and freshly cracked black pepper to taste

TO PREPARE THE RAISINS: In a small saucepan, heat the Vin Santo
over medium heat just until it boils. Add the raisins and stir until they are
well coated. Remove the pan from the heat and let sit 10 to 15 minutes
to allow the raisins to absorb the liquid and flavor of the Vin Santo.

In a medium saucepan, heat the olive oil over medium heat until hot
but not smoking. Add the eggplant, onion, and celery and cook, stirring, until
the vegetables are soft but not browned. Remove to a mixing bowl. Add the
raisins with their liquid. Add the eggplant pesto, sun-dried tomato pesto, capers,
pine nuts, garlic, parsley, and vinegar. Fold gently to combine. Add salt and pepper.

Serve warm or at room temperature as a bruschetta topping.

SERVES 4

WHITE BEAN AND TOMATO BRUSCHETTA

*Bruschetta is a traditional Italian garlic bread made
by toasting slices of baguette-style bread, rubbing them with garlic, and then
drizzling them with extra virgin olive oil. This easy-to-prepare white
bean bruschetta topping is my favorite summer snack.
It can also be transformed into a delicious light summer salad, served
with Italian canned tuna over arugula greens.*

One 16-ounce can cannellini beans (or 1½ cups cooked), drained
1 cup diced tomatoes ✹ ⅓ cup chopped red onion
2 tablespoons torn or thinly sliced fresh basil
1 teaspoon chopped fresh garlic

FOR THE VINAIGRETTE:
2 tablespoons BELLA CUCINA Sun-Dried Tomato Pesto
2 tablespoons red wine vinegar
1 tablespoon balsamic vinegar ✹ 1 tablespoon kosher salt
⅛ teaspoon freshly cracked black pepper
½ cup BELLA CUCINA Extra Virgin Olive Oil

❧

In a medium bowl, gently combine the beans,
tomatoes, onion, basil, and garlic.

TO PREPARE THE VINAIGRETTE: In a separate bowl, whisk together
all of the vinaigrette ingredients except the olive oil. While continuing
to whisk, add the olive oil in a slow, steady stream until the
mixture is emulsified. Pour the vinaigrette over the bean mixture and
toss gently until just mixed. Top the bruschetta slices with the
bean and tomato mixture and serve.

SERVES 6

CITRUS-MARINATED GRILLED SHRIMP
WITH PRESERVED ORANGE AIOLI

*This fresh citrus marinade—made with a nice balance of the slightly
sweet and acidic flavors from the preserved oranges and kumquats—accentuates
the flavor of the shrimp when grilled. The shrimp can also be
pan-sautéed over high heat, but I like the smokey flavor from cooking
over hardwood coals. As a refreshing substitute for the oranges
and kumquats, use Bella Cucina Preserved Lemons
and Sicilian Lemon Aromatic Oil as alternative ingredients.*

FOR THE CITRUS MARINADE:

2 slices BELLA CUCINA Preserved Oranges

3 preserved kumquats from a jar of BELLA CUCINA Preserved Oranges

1 tablespoon syrup from a jar of BELLA CUCINA Preserved Oranges

2 large cloves garlic ❀ 1 teaspoon kosher salt

⅛ teaspoon freshly cracked black pepper

¼ cup BELLA CUCINA Extra Virgin Olive Oil

1 pound medium shrimp, peeled with tails on

FOR PRESERVED ORANGE AIOLI:

2 tablespoons citrus marinade

1 egg yolk

1 teaspoon BELLA CUCINA Balsamic Mustard

1 tablespoon freshly squeezed lemon juice

1 large clove garlic

¾ cup BELLA CUCINA Extra Virgin Olive Oil

4 tablespoons BELLA CUCINA Mediterranean
Tangerine Aromatic Oil

TO PREPARE THE MARINADE: In a blender process
all of the marinade ingredients until coarsely chopped.
Set aside 2 tablespoons of marinade for the aioli.

Toss the shrimp with remaining marinade;
refrigerate up to two hours.

TO PREPARE THE AIOLI: In a blender process the reserved
marinade, egg yolk, mustard, lemon juice, and garlic until well
combined. While the blender is running, very slowly drizzle in the
olive oil until the sauce thickens to a mayonnaise-like consistency.
Keep aioli refrigerated until ready to use, up to two days.

Remove the shrimp from the marinade. Bring grill or sauté
pan to medium-high heat and cook shrimp on one side until pink,
about 1 to 2 minutes. Turn shrimp over and cook until
second side is pink, about 1 to 2 minutes. Serve as an antipasti
with the preserved orange aioli on the side.

SERVES 6

GRILLED SCALLOP SPIEDINI WITH PRESERVED LEMON CREAM VINAIGRETTE

This dish is so easy, and the grilled scallops on skewers make a wonderfully elegant presentation for a quick antipasti or alfresco dinner. The grilling makes it a great summer dish, but it is just as flavorful any time of the year when pan sautéed. The aromatic herbs and creamy lemon vinaigrette liven up the dish and give the scallops a velvety texture.

FOR THE VINAIGRETTE:

1 wedge BELLA CUCINA Preserved Lemon
(rinsed, pulp removed and discarded, and diced)

Juice of one lemon ✳ 1 teaspoon kosher salt

⅛ teaspoon freshly cracked black pepper

1 clove garlic, chopped

1 tablespoon chopped chives

4 tablespoons BELLA CUCINA Extra Virgin Olive Oil

4 tablespoons BELLA CUCINA Sicilian Lemon Aromatic Oil

1½ pounds medium-sized scallops *(about 24)*

½ cup BELLA CUCINA Preserved Lemon Cream

1 tablespoon BELLA CUCINA Fresh Basil Pesto

½ medium fennel bulb, cut into ¼-inch slices

4 wedges BELLA CUCINA Preserved Lemon
(rinse wedges and remove and discard pulp; cut rinds into ¼-inch slices)

12 bay leaves *(use fresh if available)*

☙

TO PREPARE THE VINAIGRETTE: In a medium mixing bowl, add the diced preserved lemon, lemon juice, salt, pepper, garlic, and chives. While whisking, add the olive oil in a slow, steady stream until the mixture is emulsified; then add the lemon oil using the same technique. Reserve two-thirds of the vinaigrette and set aside. Toss the remaining one-third of the vinaigrette with the scallops until well coated. Cover, refrigerate, and let marinate at least 30 minutes or up to 2 hours.

In a blender, add reserved vinaigrette, preserved lemon cream, and basil pesto. Blend until smooth and creamy. Set aside until ready to use.

Skewer the marinated scallops on bay leaf branches or rosemary branches with the leaves removed. *(Alternatively, use wooden or bamboo skewers. To prevent them from burning, soak skewers 30 minutes prior to skewering.)* Slide a scallop on to a skewer, then a slice of fennel, a preserved lemon, and a bay leaf. Repeat, placing 4 scallops on each skewer. *(Alternatively, use one scallop per skewer and serve as a miniature antipasti.)*

Bring grill to medium heat and cook spiedini until scallops are translucent but still tender to the touch *(about 2 minutes per side)*.

Serve warm or at room temperature with the reserved vinaigrette poured over the skewers or used as a dipping sauce.

SERVES 4

GRILLED FIGS WITH PROSCIUTTO
AND CHESTNUT HONEY

*Lightly cooking ripe figs brings out their
jam-like intensity, and combining them with the prosciutto
in this recipe creates a glorious salty-sweet marriage
of flavors. These grilled figs are also a delicious side dish
for grilled quail or insalata greens.
I like to serve them as a dessert with a slice of
dolci di latte gorgonzola cheese.*

———— ·•· ————

8 ripe figs, cut in half lengthwise through their stems

1 tablespoon BELLA CUCINA Extra Virgin Olive Oil

Kosher salt and freshly cracked black pepper

8 slices prosciutto, cut in half lengthwise

2 tablespoons chestnut honey

☙

Brush the fig slices with the olive oil and sprinkle
with salt and pepper. Prepare a low fire and grill the figs,
flesh-side down, about 8 to 10 inches from the coals,
until they are marked and begin to soften
but are not falling apart. Wrap each fig half with a
strip of prosciutto. Arrange four fig halves on each of
four plates and drizzle with chestnut honey.

SERVES 4

Olive buds are yet miniscule
next to silvery gray leaves clinging to craggy

{ *tendril branches centuries-old.* }

History gives us hope for another
fruitful harvest,
another year of life.

Dal Forno

from
THE OVEN

PANE (BASIC BREAD DOUGH)

SUN-DRIED TOMATO, GOAT CHEESE
AND ARUGULA PIZZETTA

ROASTED EGGPLANT AND FETA PIZZETTA

OLIVADA, CARAMELIZED ONION,
AND GOAT CHEESE PIZZETTA

FRESH BASIL, TOMATO, AND
PINE NUT PIZZETTA

OLIVE FOCACCIA

SWEET VIDALIA AND GOLDEN
RAISIN FOCACCIA

WALNUT SAGE, POTATO, AND
PANCETTA FOCACCIA

FOUR CHEESE AND ITALIAN SAUSAGE
CALZONE WITH ROASTED SWEET PEPPER SAUCE

ORANGE RICOTTA SCHIACCIATA

PEAR DOLCI DI LATTE SCHIACCIATA

GRAPE, GORGONZOLA, AND
CARAMELIZED WALNUT SCHIACCIATA

PANE
BASIC BREAD DOUGH

This versatile and easy-to-make dough is perfect for all types of breads, including *focaccia, calzone, pizza, and schiacciata,* and works for all of the recipes in this chapter.

I love to make this dough and prepare the topping the day before guests arrive so all I have to do is assemble the dish and put it in the oven. This allows me more time with my guests and less last-minute stress in the kitchen.

All the recipes cook beautifully in a conventional oven, but a pizza stone or seasoned brick tiles make a tremendous difference in the texture of the crust. If you fall in love with these recipes, I highly recommend investing a few dollars in one of these cooking tools.

This dough can be made by hand in a large mixing bowl or in a stand mixer with the dough hook.

The first key to the success of this dough is to use fresh yeast *(check use-by date on the package).* The second key is to bring the water used for proofing the yeast to the right temperature: warm enough but not too hot to kill the yeast (about 105° to 115°F is the desired range).

———— ·—·— ————

1⅓ tablespoons active dry yeast

2¼ cups warm water (105° to 115°F)

5 cups bread flour

1⅓ tablespoons kosher salt

OPTIONAL: 1 tablespoon chopped fresh herbs
(such as rosemary, thyme, or sage)

¼ cup BELLA CUCINA Extra Virgin Olive Oil

☙

Place yeast and warm water in a small bowl
and let sit 5 minutes, or until yeast begins to bubble,
indicating that it has been activated.

In a large bowl or in the bowl of a stand mixer, combine
the bread flour, salt, and optional herbs. Pour the yeast-and-water
mixture into the bowl. Using either a large spoon or a stand
mixer on low speed, combine the ingredients until the dough is
elastic and the bowl becomes warm. If kneading by hand,
drizzle in the olive oil in small increments. If using
a stand mixer, slowly drizzle in the olive oil while gradually
increasing the speed from low to medium. For both
methods, continue to knead or mix until the dough is smooth
and elastic *(about 10 minutes by hand, less with a stand mixer).*

Place the dough in an oiled bowl and turn to coat all sides.
Cover with a damp towel and let rest in a warm place
until dough has risen and doubled in size, about one hour.
If not using immediately, dough can be refrigerated up to
two days. Roll out according to recipe directions.

MAKES APPROXIMATELY 2½ POUNDS

SUN-DRIED TOMATO, GOAT CHEESE, AND ARUGULA PIZZETTA

1 recipe Pane *(Basic Bread Dough, page 16)*

1 bunch arugula greens

3 tablespoons BELLA CUCINA Extra Virgin Olive Oil

1 teaspoon kosher salt ❋ ⅛ teaspoon freshly cracked black pepper

One 6-ounce jar BELLA CUCINA Sun-Dried Tomato Pesto

4 ounces sun-dried tomatoes packed in oil

¾ cup freshly grated Parmigiano-Reggiano

❧

Punch prepared Pane dough down and turn out on to a
lightly floured surface. Divide into 6 equal pieces and roll each into
a ball. Roll out each ball of dough into a disk about 8 inches in
diameter and place on an oiled, parchment-lined sheetpan. Cover
sheetpan with a damp towel and let rest 45 minutes.

PREHEAT OVEN TO 425°F.
Wash and dry arugula. In a sauté pan, heat the olive oil
over medium-high heat. Add arugula, salt, and pepper and sauté until
just wilted. Remove from heat and set aside until ready to use.

Top each pizzetta with 2 tablespoons of sun-dried tomato pesto,
using entire jar. Drain the oil from the sun-dried tomatoes and place about
4 to 6 slices on each. Divide arugula and place on each pizzetta.

*Bake 45 to 50 minutes, or until crust is golden. Remove from oven
and top with Parmigiano-Reggiano. Serve warm.*

SERVES 6

ROASTED EGGPLANT AND FETA PIZZETTA

1 recipe Pane *(Basic Bread Dough, page 16)*

¼ cup BELLA CUCINA Extra Virgin Olive Oil

2 cups diced eggplant

1 teaspoon kosher salt

¼ teaspoon freshly cracked black pepper

One 6-ounce jar BELLA CUCINA Roasted Eggplant Pesto

8 ounces crumbled feta cheese

2 tablespoons chopped fresh oregano

2 tablespoons chopped fresh mint

❧

Punch prepared Pane dough down and turn out on to a lightly
floured surface. Divide into 6 equal pieces and roll each into a ball.
Roll out each ball of dough into a disk about 8 inches in diameter,
and place on an oiled, parchment-lined sheetpan.
Cover sheetpan with a damp towel and let rest 45 minutes.

PREHEAT OVEN TO 425°F.
Heat olive oil in a sauté pan over medium heat. Add diced eggplant,
salt, and pepper and sauté 5 minutes, until softened.

Top each pizzetta with 2 tablespoons of eggplant pesto,
using entire jar. Top with the sautéed diced eggplant and crumbled
feta cheese. Mix herbs together and sprinkle on the pizzetta.

*Bake 45 to 50 minutes, or until crust is golden brown.
Remove from oven. Serve warm.*

SERVES 6

OLIVADA, CARAMELIZED ONION, AND GOAT CHEESE PIZZETTA

1 recipe Pane (*Basic Bread Dough, page 16*)
FOR THE CARAMELIZED ONIONS:
2 tablespoons BELLA CUCINA Extra Virgin Olive Oil
1 tablespoon butter ✤ 1 red onion, cut into half-moon slices
1 tablespoon red wine vinegar

One 6-ounce jar BELLA CUCINA Olivada Olive Pesto
1 cup BELLA CUCINA Antipasti Olives, pitted ✤ 8 ounces goat cheese, crumbled
2 tablespoons chopped fresh oregano

❧

Punch prepared Pane dough down and turn out on to a
lightly floured surface. Divide into 6 equal pieces and roll each into a ball.
Roll out each ball of dough into a disk about 8 inches in diameter and place
on an oiled, parchment-lined sheetpan. Cover sheetpan with a
damp towel and let rest 45 minutes.

TO PREPARE CARAMELIZED ONIONS: In a sauté pan, heat butter
and olive oil over medium-low heat until the butter foams. Add the onions
and cook until soft and translucent (*about 10 minutes*). Add the red wine
vinegar and cook until the liquid is almost absorbed, about 20 minutes.

PREHEAT OVEN TO 425°F.
Top each pizzetta with 2 tablespoons pesto, using entire jar. Divide caramelized
onions among the pizzettas and spread them evenly over the dough. Cut the olives
in half and place on top of the onions. Top with goat cheese and oregano.

Bake 45 to 50 minutes, or until crust is golden brown.
Remove from oven. Serve warm.

SERVES 6

FRESH BASIL, TOMATO, AND PINE NUT PIZZETTA

1 recipe Pane (*Basic Bread Dough, page 16*)
2 tablespoons balsamic vinegar
Kosher salt and freshly cracked black pepper to taste
3 tablespoons Bella Cucina Mediterranean Tangerine Aromatic Oil
1 pint cherry tomatoes, cut in half
One 6-ounce jar Bella Cucina Fresh Basil Pesto
8 ounces fresh mozzarella ✤ 6 tablespoons pine nuts
1 cup torn fresh basil leaves ✤ ¾ cup Parmigiano-Reggiano

❧

Punch prepared Pane dough down and turn out on to a
lightly floured surface. Divide into 6 equal pieces and roll each into
a ball. Roll out each ball of dough into a disk about 8 inches in
diameter and place on an oiled, parchment-lined sheetpan. Cover
sheetpan with a damp towel and let rest 45 minutes.

PREHEAT OVEN TO 425°F.
In a small bowl, combine vinegar, salt, and pepper. Whisk in oil until well-combined.
Toss cherry tomatoes with the vinaigrette. Set aside to marinate until ready to use.

Top each pizzetta with 2 tablespoons pesto, using entire jar. Cut mozzarella
into 12 slices and place 2 slices on each pizzetta. Remove tomatoes
from the vinaigrette with a slotted spoon and divide among the pizzettas. Reserve
vinaigrette for use when pizzettas are cooked. Sprinkle pine nuts on pizzettas.

Bake 45 to 50 minutes, or until crust is golden brown.
Remove from oven. Drizzle each pizzetta with the remaining vinaigrette
and top with fresh basil leaves and Parmigiano-Reggiano.

SERVES 6

OLIVE FOCACCIA

*This traditional combination of olives, sea salt, and
fresh rosemary is a classic Mediterranean favorite. Try making different
shapes and sizes with the dough for an interesting presentation.*

1 recipe Pane (*Basic Bread Dough, page 16*)
½ cup BELLA CUCINA Extra Virgin Olive Oil
1 cup BELLA CUCINA Antipasti Olives, pitted
1 tablespoon sea salt or kosher salt
2 tablespoons rosemary needles

❧

Punch prepared Pane dough down and turn out on to a lightly
floured surface. Roll into an 11-by-16-inch rectangle. Place on an oiled
sheetpan and press dough to the edges to fill the pan. (*You can use a smaller sheetpan,
but the cooking time may need to be adjusted based on the increased thickness of the dough.*)
Cover sheetpan with a damp towel and let rest 45 minutes.

PREHEAT OVEN TO 425°F.
Brush dough with 6 tablespoons olive oil. Make indentations
in the dough with your fingertips and place the olives in the impressions.
Sprinkle the dough evenly with salt and rosemary.

Bake 45 to 50 minutes or until crust is golden brown.
Remove from the oven and drizzle with the remaining 2 tablespoons oil.

SERVES 12

SWEET VIDALIA AND GOLDEN RAISIN FOCACCIA

*This savory and sweet focaccia is perfect as an appetizer
served before dinner with a chilled glass of Prosecco or Pinot Grigio.
The Vin Santo plumps up the raisins and adds
an intense flavor and texture.*

1 recipe Pane (*Basic Bread Dough, page 16*)
½ cup Vin Santo
1 cup golden raisins
1 jar BELLA CUCINA Sweet Vidalia Onion Pesto
2 tablespoons thyme leaves
2 tablespoons BELLA CUCINA Extra Virgin Olive Oil

❧

Punch prepared Pane dough down and turn out on to a lightly floured
surface. Roll into a 11-by-16-inch rectangle. Place on an oiled sheetpan and
press dough to the edges to fill the pan. (*You can use a smaller sheetpan, but
the cooking time may need to be adjusted based on the increased thickness of the dough.*)
Cover sheetpan with a damp towel and let rest 45 minutes.

PREHEAT OVEN TO 425°F.
In small saucepan, heat Vin Santo until just boiling.
Add the raisins and turn until coated. Remove pan from heat
and set aside until ready to use.

Spoon vidalia onion pesto over dough in an even layer.
Bake 20 minutes. Remove focaccia from oven and sprinkle plumped
raisins, juice from raisins, and fresh thyme evenly over onion layer.
Put focaccia back in oven to finish cooking, about 15 to 20 minutes,
or until edges of focaccia dough are golden brown. Brush edges
of dough with olive oil. Cool slightly before cutting.

SERVES 12

WALNUT SAGE, POTATO, AND PANCETTA FOCACCIA

I love the complex flavor combination in this savory recipe.
When available at your grocer or local farmer's market, use Yukon Gold,
yellow fin or fingerling potatoes for the creamiest flavor and texture.

1 recipe Pane (*Basic Bread Dough, page 16*)
1 pound Yukon Gold potatoes
1 jar BELLA CUCINA Walnut Sage Pesto
2 tablespoons Parmigiano-Reggiano
8 fresh sage leaves ✺ 4 ounces thinly sliced pancetta
1 tablespoon kosher salt
2 tablespoons BELLA CUCINA Extra Virgin Olive Oil

❦

Punch prepared Pane dough down and turn out on to a lightly floured
surface. Roll into a 11-by-16-inch rectangle. Place on an oiled sheetpan and
press dough to the edges to fill the pan. (*You can use a smaller sheetpan, but
the cooking time may need to be adjusted based on the increased thickness of the dough.*)
Cover sheetpan with a damp towel and let rest 45 minutes.

Boil unpeeled potatoes in salted water just until they can be easily
pierced with a knife, about 15 minutes. Drain and set aside until cool
enough to handle. Once cool, cut crosswise into ¼-inch slices;
set aside until ready to use.

PREHEAT OVEN TO 425°F.
Spread walnut sage pesto evenly on focaccia dough.
Place pancetta over the pesto in an even layer and top with the potatoes.
Sprinkle with Parmigiano-Reggiano, sage leaves, and salt.

Bake 45 to 50 minutes or until dough is golden brown on edges and top.
Rotate the pan halfway through the cooking time for even baking. Remove from the
oven and brush edges of dough with olive oil. Cool slightly before cutting.

SERVES 12

FOUR CHEESE AND ITALIAN SAUSAGE CALZONE WITH ROASTED SWEET PEPPER SAUCE

This recipe can be served as a savory, casual antipasti or, depending
on the size of calzone you make, a first or main course.
Kids love this dish, which is really just a folded pizza. The combination
of the cheeses melts deliciously into the dough.
For a vegetarian version, substitute sautéed spinach or Swiss chard
greens for the sausage. There are lots of delicious flavor combinations:
use your imagination to create your own favorite calzone.

———————

1 recipe Pane (*Basic Bread Dough, page 16*)

½ pound mild Italian sausage meat or links (*about 2 sausages*)

2 ounces fresh mozzarella, cut into ½-inch cubes

2 ounces fontina cheese, grated ✽ 1 ounce Parmigiano-Reggiano, grated

6 ounces goat cheese, crumbled

2 tablespoons chopped fresh Italian flat-leaf parsley

½ cup roasted red peppers, diced

¼ cup BELLA CUCINA Fresh Basil Pesto

2 tablespoons fresh basil, chopped

2 tablespoons fresh oregano, chopped ✽ 1 teaspoon kosher salt

¼ teaspoon freshly cracked black pepper

¼ cup BELLA CUCINA Extra Virgin Olive Oil

One 6-ounce jar BELLA CUCINA Sweet Pepper Pesto

❧

Punch prepared Pane dough down and turn out on to a lightly
floured surface. Cut dough into twelve 2-ounce pieces and roll into balls
(you will have leftover dough). Roll each dough ball into a flat disk
about 6 inches in diameter and place them on an an oiled sheetpan.
Cover sheetpan with a damp towel and let rest 45 minutes.

PREHEAT OVEN TO 425°F.
Remove and discard the sausage casings. Break the meat into
pieces over a large bowl. Add mozzarella, fontina, Parmigiano-Reggiano,
goat cheese, parsley, roasted red peppers, basil pesto,
fresh basil, oregano, salt, and black pepper. Toss ingredients
by hand or with a spoon until combined.

Refrigerate sausage mixture until ready to use
(*may be prepared up to 2 days in advance*).

Place 2 tablespoons of the sausage mixture in the center of each disk.
Brush the inside edge of the dough with water and fold it over into a half-moon
shape. Seal edges of the dough by gently pressing edges together,
crimping them, and then folding edges over. Brush the tops with olive oil.

Bake 45 to 55 minutes or until the dough is golden brown.
Remove from oven and brush with olive oil again.

Heat the sweet pepper pesto and serve warm as
a dipping sauce on the side.

MAKES 12 SMALL CALZONES

ORANGE RICOTTA SCHIACCIATA

*This surprising combination of flavors is a
delicious breakfast or dessert flatbread. The orange flower
water in the syrup of the preserved oranges and the richness
of the chestnut honey add a wonderful aromatic
and floral complement to the mild ricotta cheese.
As always, it's worth the effort to seek out fresh ricotta
from a local specialty market.*

½ recipe Pane (*Basic Bread Dough, page 16*)
1 pound (2 cups) ricotta cheese
¼ cup syrup from BELLA CUCINA Preserved Oranges
½ cup BELLA CUCINA Preserved Oranges, chopped
¼ cup sugar
2 tablespoons thinly sliced mint leaves for garnish

Roll out dough on to a floured surface into an
11-by-16-inch rectangle. Place on an oiled sheetpan and press
dough to the edges to fill the pan. (*You can use a smaller
sheetpan, but the cooking time may need to be adjusted based on
the increased thickness of the dough.*) Cover sheetpan
with a damp towel and let rest 45 minutes.

PREHEAT OVEN TO 425°F.
In a small bowl, combine the ricotta and the syrup
from the oranges. Spread ricotta mixture evenly over
dough, leaving 1 inch around the edge. Scatter oranges
and sprinkle sugar over the ricotta layer.

Bake 40 to 45 minutes or until the edges of the dough
are browned. Remove from the oven and sprinkle
with mint. Cool slightly before cutting.

SERVES 10

Pear Dolci di Latte Schiacciata

*This flatbread won't last long once it comes
out of the oven. Enjoy it as an afternoon snack with
a glass of Vin Santo.*

½ recipe Pane *(Basic Bread Dough, page 16)*

½ cup mascarpone cheese

½ cup sugar

2 large Bosc or Bartlett pears, fresh or poached, *(recipe page 89)*

½ cup Bella Cucina Dolci di Latte Caramel Sauce

Punch prepared Pane dough down and turn out
on to a lightly floured surface.

Roll into an 11-by-16-inch rectangle. Place on an oiled
sheetpan and press dough to the edges to fill the pan. *(You can use
a smaller sheetpan, but the cooking time may need to be adjusted based
on the increased thickness of the dough.)* Cover sheetpan with a
damp towel and let rest 45 minutes.

Preheat oven to 425°f.
In a small bowl, combine mascarpone and sugar.
Spoon cheese mixture evenly over dough, leaving 1 inch uncovered
around the edges. Peel, core, and slice pears into ¼-inch pieces and
place in fan-like presentation on top of the mascarpone.

Bake 40 to 45 minutes or until the edges of the dough are brown.
While the schiacciata is cooking, heat the caramel sauce in a pan or in the
microwave. When the schiacciata is done, remove it from the oven
and drizzle with caramel sauce. Cool slightly before cutting.

Serves 10

GRAPE, GORGONZOLA, AND CARAMELIZED WALNUT SCHIACCIATA

This unusual combination is actually an adaptation of the traditional flatbread made during the autumn grape harvest. Typically, it is made as a stuffed bread, but I prefer this version because the taste of the grapes and its juices are the predominant flavors.

½ recipe Pane *(Basic Bread Dough, page 16)*

FOR THE CARAMELIZED WALNUTS:

½ cup butter

½ cup walnut halves, toasted

1 teaspoons sugar

½ cup red wine

½ cup sugar

2 cups red seedless grapes *(red flame or any other variety)*

½ cup BELLA CUCINA Cranberry Conserve

4 ounces Dolci di Latte gorgonzola cheese *(or any other blue cheese)*

Punch prepared Pane dough down
and turn out on to a lightly floured surface.

Roll into an 11-by-16-inch rectangle. Place on an oiled
sheetpan and press dough to the edges to fill the pan.
*(You can use a smaller sheetpan, but the cooking time may need to be adjusted
based on the increased thickness of the dough.)* Cover sheetpan with
a damp towel and let rest 45 minutes.

TO PREPARE CARAMELIZED WALNUTS: Heat butter
in a sauté pan over low heat until melted, bubbly, and
light brown. Add walnuts and sugar and stir until walnuts are
well-coated and have a caramel-like texture and color.
Place the walnuts on a buttered sheetpan and let cool.

Heat wine and sugar over medium heat until the
sugar is dissolved and the mixture is thick and syrupy, about
5 to 7 minutes. Remove from heat and toss with grapes
until well coated. Set aside until ready to use.

PREHEAT OVEN TO 425°F.
Spread cranberry conserve on the dough in an even layer.
Make indentations with your fingertips and scatter the grapes on
the dough. Drizzle with the wine-and-sugar syrup.
Bake 30 minutes. Remove schiacciata from oven and top
with gorgonzola and walnuts. Continue baking an additional
15 to 20 minutes, until the edges of the dough are
golden brown. Cool slightly before cutting.

SERVES 10

Insalate

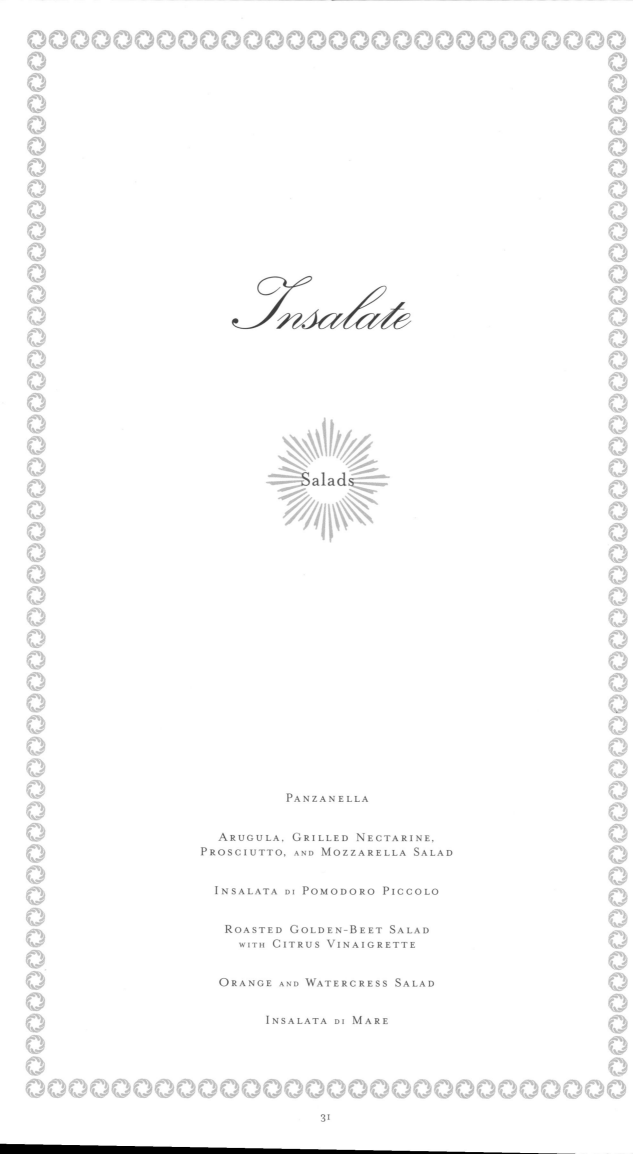

Salads

PANZANELLA

ARUGULA, GRILLED NECTARINE,
PROSCIUTTO, AND MOZZARELLA SALAD

INSALATA DI POMODORO PICCOLO

ROASTED GOLDEN-BEET SALAD
WITH CITRUS VINAIGRETTE

ORANGE AND WATERCRESS SALAD

INSALATA DI MARE

My philosophy about food is cradled
somewhere between
the earth & the table
and everything in between.

PANZANELLA

This recipe is one of my summer favorites.
Traditionally, panzanella is made with leftover bread that has dried
out, been soaked in water to rehydrate it, and then squeezed
of its liquid. I prefer the extra flavor, crunch, and texture you
get from using focaccia croutons. Add grilled
chicken breast to the panzanella for a heartier salad.

FOR THE FOCACCIA CROUTONS:

1 loaf focaccia bread, cut into one-inch squares *(about 4 cups)*
8 tablespoons BELLA CUCINA Extra Virgin Olive Oil

FOR THE SALAD:

1 cup diced English cucumber

½ cup diced red onion

½ cup sliced radish *(optional)*

1 cup BELLA CUCINA Antipasti Olives, pitted and halved

1 cup halved yellow and cherry tomatoes, or diced tomatoes

1 cup diced fresh milk mozzarella

¼ cup torn fresh basil leaves

FOR THE VINAIGRETTE:

½ cup red wine vinegar

4 tablespoons BELLA CUCINA Olivada Olive Pesto

1 tablespoon kosher salt

1 teaspoon freshly cracked black pepper

¾ cup BELLA CUCINA Extra Virgin Olive Oil

4 tablespoons BELLA CUCINA Mediterranean Tangerine Aromatic Oil

TO PREPARE FOCCACIA CROUTONS:
Toss bread cubes with olive oil until well-coated.
Toast in 350°F oven until browned, about 20 minutes.

TO PREPARE THE SALAD : In a large bowl, toss together all the salad
ingredients and the focaccia croutons until just combined.

TO PREPARE THE VINAIGRETTE: In a medium bowl,
whisk together the vinegar, olive pesto, salt, and pepper.
While continuing to whisk, add the olive and tangerine oils in
a slow, steady stream; whisk until mixture is emulsified.

Pour the vinaigrette over the salad and toss gently
to combine. Let sit 5 to 10 minutes, until the vinaigrette
is absorbed and the croutons begin to soften.

SERVES 6

ARUGULA, GRILLED NECTARINE, PROSCIUTTO, AND MOZZARELLA SALAD

A bite of this salad is like eating a slice of summer.
I love how simple and refreshing it is, and also the elegance of
its unique presentation and combination of ingredients.
Other seasonal fruits, such as figs, peaches, and apricots, can
be easily substituted for the ones listed below.

———— ·•·· ————

2 ripe nectarines

2 tablespoons BELLA CUCINA Extra Virgin Olive Oil

1 teaspoon kosher salt

FOR THE VINAIGRETTE:

1 tablespoon chestnut honey

1 tablespoon red wine vinegar

1 tablespoon balsamic vinegar ✻ 1 teaspoon kosher salt

4 tablespoons BELLA CUCINA Extra Virgin Olive Oil

4 tablespoons BELLA CUCINA
Mediterranean Tangerine Aromatic Oil

❦

1 bunch arugula greens

4 slices prosciutto *(about 2 ounces)*

4 ounces fresh milk mozzarella
(pulled apart by hand into bite size pieces)

10 to 12 fresh mint leaves, torn

Freshly cracked black pepper to taste

❦

Cut nectarines into thick slices. Rub with olive oil
and gently toss or brush with salt. Grill until just soft
and marked, about 30 seconds per side.

TO PREPARE VINAIGRETTE: In a mixing bowl, whisk together
the chestnut honey, red wine and balsamic vinegars, and
kosher salt. While continuing to whisk, add the olive oil, then
the tangerine aromatic oil, in a slow, steady stream
until the mixture is emulsified.

Spread the arugula on a platter, draping prosciutto
slices over the leaves. Top with the grilled nectarine slices and
mozzarella. Drizzle the vinaigrette over the salad and top with
the torn mint leaves and freshly cracked black pepper.

SERVES 4

Insalata di Pomodoro Piccolo

*I love summer foods. The harvest from our backyard
garden and Saturday organic farmer's market inspire my menu.
The dizzying variety of seasonal fresh fruits and vegetables makes
my cooking fast, easy, and deliciously simple. It takes very little work
to combine seasonal offerings into colorful creations.
I love returning each week to see what each farmer is harvesting
as the summer progresses. This "little tomato salad" is a summer favorite
at my house. It highlights small heirloom varietals while they are
at their peak of ripeness and offers a burst of summer flavor with every bite.
If these smaller varieties are not available, any size or variety will
make for a delicious presentation.*

---

1 pound small vine-ripened tomatoes
(*use any combination of small tomatoes that look good:
red and golden sweet 100, cherry, or plum*)

8 ounces bocconcini mozzarella balls

2 tablespoons fresh piccolo variety basil leaves,
or torn fresh basil leaves

1 tablespoon BELLA CUCINA Cabernet Vinegar

Kosher salt and freshly cracked black pepper to taste

3 tablespoons BELLA CUCINA Mediterranean Tangerine Aromatic Oil

⌘

Halve or slice the tomatoes, depending on their size, and
combine them with the mozzarella and basil in a large bowl.

In a separate, small bowl, add the vinegar, salt, and pepper.
While whisking, add the tangerine oil to the small bowl in a slow,
steady stream and whisk until the mixture is emulsified.

Pour the vinaigrette over the tomatoes and serve.

SERVES 4

ROASTED GOLDEN-BEET SALAD WITH CITRUS VINAIGRETTE

I always look forward to making this salad when the season's first golden beets appear at the market. Oven roasting enhances their color and sweetness. If you can't find golden beets, look for chiogga beets. Young, tender beets work best with this salad.

---

1 pound golden beets, trimmed and cleaned

2 tablespoons BELLA CUCINA Extra Virgin Olive Oil

3 large cloves garlic, crushed in their skins

3 sprigs fresh thyme

2 tablespoons freshly squeezed blood orange or navel orange juice

1 tablespoon balsamic vinegar

1 tablespoon BELLA CUCINA Cabernet Vinegar

Kosher salt and freshly cracked black pepper to taste

6 tablespoons BELLA CUCINA Mediterranean Tangerine Aromatic Oil

1 bunch arugula greens, trimmed of stems, washed and dried

PREHEAT OVEN TO 350°F.
Place the beets in a large ovenproof dish. Drizzle with the
olive oil and scatter the garlic and thyme in the dish.
Cover with foil and roast until the beets can be pierced easily
with a knife, about 50 to 60 minutes. Remove from the oven and
let cool. Discard thyme. Remove garlic from skillet and reserve.
When the beets are cool, peel and discard the skins.
Cut beets in half, then slice them into half-moons.

In a mixing bowl, whisk together the orange juice,
balsamic and cabernet vinegars, reserved garlic, and salt
and pepper. While continuing to whisk, add first
the olive oil, then the tangerine aromatic oil, in a slow,
steady stream. Whisk until the mixture is emulsified.

Gently toss the beets with two-thirds
of the vinaigrette; let marinate 15 minutes.

In a large bowl, toss the arugula with the remaining
vinaigrette until the greens are just coated.

Divide the arugula among four serving plates.
Arrange the sliced beets atop the greens and serve.

SERVES 4

ORANGE AND WATERCRESS SALAD

*This recipe is an adaptation of a traditional
Sicilian salad, combining sweet and tart flavors from the oranges
and the red wine vinegar. Try it as a refreshing side dish
or as a base for a roasted chicken salad.*

FOR THE CARAMELIZED ONIONS:
1 tablespoon butter
2 tablespoons BELLA CUCINA Extra Virgin Olive Oil
1 red onion, cut into half-moon slices
1 tablespoon red wine vinegar

FOR THE VINAIGRETTE:
¼ cup freshly squeezed orange juice *(about 1 orange)*
1 tablespoon syrup from BELLA CUCINA Preserved Oranges
1 teaspoon BELLA CUCINA Cabernet Vinegar
1 teaspoon balsamic vinegar
½ teaspoon kosher salt
⅛ teaspoon freshly cracked black pepper
⅓ cup BELLA CUCINA Extra Virgin Olive Oil

1 blood orange *(use a navel orange or tangerine
if blood oranges are not available)*
¼ cup coarsely chopped BELLA CUCINA Preserved Oranges

FOR THE SALAD:
1 bunch watercress, thick stems removed and discarded
¼ cup BELLA CUCINA Antipasti Olives, pitted

❧

TO PREPARE CARAMELIZED ONIONS: In a sauté pan,
heat the butter and olive oil over medium-low heat until the
butter foams. Add the onion and cook until soft and translucent
(about 10 minutes). Add the red wine vinegar and cook until
the liquid is almost absorbed.

TO PREPARE THE VINAIGRETTE: In a medium bowl, whisk together
all of the vinaigrette ingredients except the olive oil. While continuing
to whisk, add the olive oil in a slow, steady stream until the
mixture is emulsified. Set aside one-quarter of the vinaigrette.

Remove and discard the orange peel; section the
orange *(don't slice it)*. Add the blood orange segments, preserved
oranges, and caramelized red onion slices to the reserved vinaigrette;
toss gently until covered. Set aside to marinate 15 minutes.

TO PREPARE THE SALAD: Wash and gently dry the watercress
and place it on a platter. Toss with just enough of the remaining
vinaigrette to coat the greens. Arrange the marinated oranges
and onion slices over the watercress.

Top with the antipasti olives and serve immediately.

SERVES 4

INSALATA DI MARE

*This seafood salad reminds me of afternoon alfresco
lunches on the seaside coast in Liguria, Italy. Fresh seafood is
always on the menu at the local cafés, highlighting the catch
of the day. If you can't find fresh calamari or octopus, the frozen
variety should be readily available from your grocer or fishmonger.
It is one of the few seafoods that can be frozen
without compromising the flavor of the dish. Of course,
as with any dish, fresh is always preferred.*

FOR THE VINAIGRETTE:

¼ wedge BELLA CUCINA Preserved Lemons, diced
(*rinse lemon and pat dry, remove and discard pulp*)

3 large cloves garlic, peeled and minced

Juice of ½ lemon

2 tablespoons champagne vinegar or white wine vinegar

¼ cup BELLA CUCINA Extra Virgin Olive Oil

2 tablespoons BELLA CUCINA Sicilian Lemon Aromatic Oil

Kosher salt and freshly cracked black pepper

FOR THE SEAFOOD:

1 pound baby octopus tentacles *(the body can also be used,
but remove and discard eyes, mouth area, and viscera)*

2½ pounds calamari bodies and heads, cleaned

alternatively, you can use all calamari

1 cup peeled and diced boiling potato

½ red pepper and ½ yellow pepper, deveined and diced

2 tablespoons drained capers, rinsed

2 tablespoons minced fresh basil leaves

TO PREPARE THE VINAIGRETTE: In a small bowl, whisk together
the diced preserved lemon rind, garlic, lemon juice, and vinegar. While
continuing to whisk, add the olive and lemon oils in a slow, steady stream,
until the mixture is emulsified. Season with salt and pepper. Set aside.

TO PREPARE THE SEAFOOD: If necessary, detach and set
aside the octopus tentacles. Cut the bodies into ½-inch rings. Slice the
calamari into ½-inch pieces. Toss fish with 2 tablespoons vinaigrette.
Over medium heat, grill the fish 1 to 2 minutes per side.

Bring a large pot of salted water to boil. Cook potatoes
until tender but not mushy. Drain and cool.

In a large bowl combine seafood, potatoes, red and yellow peppers, capers,
basil, and vinaigrette. Toss to coat. Drizzle with lemon oil.

SERVES 4

Zuppa

{ Soups }

SUMMER VEGETABLE
MINESTRONE WITH BASIL PESTO

FENNEL AND TOMATO SOUP
WITH ARBORIO RICE

PESCE EN BRODO
WITH SAFFRON RISOTTO

SWEET ONION, WILD MUSHROOM,
AND FARRO SOUP

VEAL STOCK

SUMMER VEGETABLE
MINESTRONE WITH BASIL PESTO

*Highlighting the garden's harvest of green vegetables in a
simple yet elegant and refreshing dish, this soup can be made quickly.
You can prepare it and be back outdoors in no time
for an alfresco lunch.*

¼ cup BELLA CUCINA Extra Virgin Olive Oil

1 cup thinly sliced leeks, well washed and drained

1 cup diced fennel

½ cup diced celery

1 tablespoon chopped fresh garlic

¼ cup white wine

4 cups vegetable or chicken stock

1 cup fresh peas when in season, or use fresh green
beans cut into 1-inch pieces

½ cup thinly sliced Swiss chard or celery leaves

Kosher salt and freshly cracked black pepper to taste

4 to 6 tablespoons BELLA CUCINA Fresh Basil Pesto

In a large saucepan, heat the olive oil over medium heat.
Reduce heat to medium-low and add leeks, fennel, celery, and garlic.
Cook, stirring, until vegetables are soft and translucent.
Be careful not to brown the vegetables.

Add the white wine to the saucepan and cook until
almost absorbed. Add the stock, bring to a simmer, and cook,
covered, 30 to 45 minutes. *(Taste the soup at 30 minutes; if a delicate
vegetable flavor has not developed, let simmer an additional 10 to 15 minutes.)*
Five minutes before serving, add the green beans and the Swiss chard.
Add salt and pepper to taste. Divide soup among four bowls
and top each serving with 1 tablespoon basil pesto.

Serve with extra pesto on the side and toasted crostini rounds.

SERVES 4

FENNEL AND TOMATO SOUP
WITH ARBORIO RICE

When you are craving the flavor of ripe tomatoes in the dead of winter, Bella Cucina Organic Passata al Pomodoro is just the thing. It's made from summer-fresh, vine-ripened Italian San Marzano tomatoes, which are pressed through a mill in order to extract all of their flavor and vitamins, without the seeds or skins.

———— ·►◄· ————

3 tablespoons BELLA CUCINA Extra Virgin Olive Oil

1 cup chopped yellow onion

1 cup thinly sliced fresh fennel

2 tablespoons chopped fresh garlic

1 tablespoon chopped fresh Italian flat-leaf parsley

1 jar BELLA CUCINA Organic Passata al Pomodoro

¼ cup chopped BELLA CUCINA Preserved Oranges

4 cups vegetable or chicken stock

Kosher salt and freshly cracked black pepper to taste

½ cup Arborio rice

2 tablespoons BELLA CUCINA Mediterranean
Tangerine Aromatic Oil

☙

In a large pot, heat the olive oil over medium heat.
Add the onion, fennel, garlic, and parsley and cook,
stirring, until soft, about 5 to 10 minutes.

Stir in passata, preserved oranges, and stock. Add salt
and pepper. Simmer, covered, for 40 to 45 minutes. Add the
rice and simmer, covered, stirring occasionally, until rice
is al dente, about 20 minutes.

Serve hot with a drizzle of tangerine oil over each serving.

SERVES 4

PESCE EN BRODO WITH SAFFRON RISOTTO

This is my version of the traditional regional fish soup made in the Mediterranean. I like a lighter style with a hint of citrus in the broth. As with any dish, the final result is only as good as the freshness of the ingredients. The key here is to use the freshest seasonal fish available at your local grocer or fishmonger. One last note: The risotto adds a depth to the meal, but the soup is delicious on its own.

FOR THE FISH BROTH:

4 ounces of a combination of fish trimmings, flesh of fish, shrimp shells, shellfish, and/or bones *(cleaned)*

½ stalk celery, cut into 1-inch pieces

½ yellow onion, cut crosswise into chunks

¼ cup white wine

6 to 8 whole black peppercorns

1 bay leaf

FOR THE SEAFOOD:

4 tablespoons BELLA CUCINA Extra Virgin Olive Oil

1 large whole garlic clove, peeled

2 cups BELLA CUCINA Organic Passata al Pomodoro

¼ cup freshly squeezed orange juice

8 ounces salmon fillets, skins removed

12 ounces white fish such as halibut, sea bass, or cod

(use any combination of what's fresh that day from your fishmonger)

½ pound fresh shrimp, shelled with tails on

½ pound shellfish, such as mussels and clams

FOR THE SAFFRON RISOTTO:

4 cups chicken or vegetable broth

3 threads of saffron, or to taste

1 tablespoon BELLA CUCINA Extra Virgin Olive Oil

1 tablespoon unsalted butter

1 medium yellow onion, chopped

1 tablespoon chopped fresh garlic ❀ 1 cup Arborio rice

Kosher salt and freshly cracked black pepper to taste

Chopped fresh basil leaves, for garnish

4 tablespoons BELLA CUCINA Sicilian Lemon Aromatic Oil

❧

TO PREPARE FISH BROTH: Place all ingredients in a saucepan
over medium heat, add 3 cups water, and bring to a boil. Reduce heat and
simmer 30 minutes. Strain broth into a bowl, pushing out all the
liquid from the fish. Discard solids; reserve broth.

TO PREPARE THE SEAFOOD: In a large saucepan with a
tight-fitting lid, heat olive oil over medium heat. Add garlic clove to pan
and sauté until it just turns a golden brown; discard garlic clove.

Stir the passata, orange juice, and fish broth into the seasoned oil and bring
the mixture to a low boil. Add the fish and shellfish, cover the pan, and cook until the
fish is just opaque and the shellfish has just opened, about 3 to 5 minutes.
(The dish will continue to cook off the heat, so do not overcook.)

TO PREPARE THE RISOTTO: In a medium saucepan,
bring the chicken or vegetable broth to a simmer. Add saffron and
stir until dissolved. Keep warm over low heat.

In large a saucepan, heat the olive oil and butter over
medium-high heat until the butter is melted. Add the onion and garlic
and sauté until soft, about 4 to 5 minutes. Add the Arborio rice
and stir until the rice is well-coated and begins to turn translucent.

Add one cup of broth to the large saucepan and stir constantly,
until the Arborio absorbs almost all of the liquid, about five minutes.
Repeat, adding broth one cup at a time until all of the
broth is gone. The process should take about 35 to 40 minutes
and the resulting rice should be creamy and al dente. Stir in
additional butter, to taste, and salt and pepper.

*To serve, ladle reserved fish broth into deep bowls and spoon the risotto into
the middle of each, then divide the cooked fish and shellfish evenly among the bowls.
Top with fresh chopped basil leaves, drizzle with lemon oil, and serve hot.*

SERVES 4

SWEET ONION, WILD MUSHROOM, AND FARRO SOUP

*I was inspired to create this recipe after a trip
to the Chiusi market in Tuscany, Italy, where just-foraged fresh
porcini mushrooms were being sold by the crateful.
It is difficult, if not impossible, to find fresh porcini in many parts of
this country. Nowadays, however, most grocers carry a variety
of fresh and dried mushrooms that can be acceptable substitutes. For a
cleaner flavor, I prefer fresh mushrooms when available.*

———————

4 tablespoons BELLA CUCINA Extra Virgin Olive Oil

5 tablespoons unsalted butter

1 cup diced carrot ❋ ¾ cup diced celery

2 tablespoons chopped Italian flat-leaf parsley

1 tablespoon chopped fresh garlic

1 pound wild mushrooms (*any combination of porcini, cremini, shitake, portobello,
or chanterelle*), brushed clean, stems trimmed if woody, and sliced

1 teaspoon kosher salt

⅛ teaspoon freshly cracked black pepper to taste

½ cup red wine ❋ 1 cup farro

One 6-ounce jar BELLA CUCINA Sweet Vidalia Onion Pesto

6 cups Veal Stock (*recipe, opposite*) or chicken,
beef, or vegetable stock or broth

FOR THE CROSTINI:

1 baguette loaf

2 tablespoons melted butter

½ cup Parmigiano-Reggiano

☙

In a large heavy saucepan over medium heat add 2 tablespoons
olive oil and 2 tablespoons butter; heat until the butter foams. Add carrots,
celery, parsley, and garlic; cook, stirring, until soft, 4 to 5 minutes.

In a small saucepan over high heat add remaining 2 tablespoons olive oil
and 2 tablespoons butter; heat until the butter foams. Add sliced mushrooms,
salt, and pepper; cook, stirring occasionally, until browned. Add red wine,
reduce heat to medium, and cook until liquid is reduced by half. Add onion
and veal stock and bring to a boil. Add farro and simmer, covered,
covered, 45 minutes, until farro is tender. Season to taste.

TO MAKE CROSTINI: PREHEAT OVEN TO 375°F;
butter a baking sheet. Slice baguette into eight ½-inch slices;
place on baking sheet. Spoon 1 tablespoon Parmigiano-Reggiano on to
each slice. Bake 10 minutes, until slightly brown.

*Ladle hot soup into bowls; place one crostini on top,
serving the rest on the side.*

SERVES 6

*In place of farro in this soup try our Mediterranean Pearl Pasta with
Porcini Mushrooms and Sage, adding a 5-ounce box where the recipe calls for farro.*

VEAL STOCK

Although the Sweet Onion, Wild Mushroom, and
Farro Soup is delicious with beef, chicken, or vegetable broth,
this quick veal stock truly enhances the flavor.
The veal bones are delicious to serve alongside the dish
(or nibble on them yourself while preparing the soup).

1½ pounds veal breast, shoulder or shank, cut into pieces

1 cup coarsely chopped yellow onion

½ cup coarsely chopped carrots

½ cup coarsely chopped celery

1 cup red wine

Handful fresh parsley stems, with or without leaves

2 bay leaves ❁ 1 teaspoon peppercorns

PREHEAT OVEN TO 375°F.
Place the veal and vegetables in a roasting pan; roast until the meat
is well browned and the vegetables have caramelized, about 20-30 minutes.

Transfer the veal and vegetables to a stockpot. Place the roasting pan
over medium-high heat and add the red wine to deglaze the pan, stirring
and scraping up the browned bits until the liquid is boiling. Add it to the
stock pot along with 8 cups water, parsley, bay leaves, and peppercorns.

Simmer uncovered for 2 to 3 hours until the flavor is rich
and the stock is dark, skimming the fat off the top and stirring regularly.
Strain the stock, discarding the vegetables and peppercorns and
reserving the veal for another use if desired.

The stock may be used immediately or refrigerated for
up to one week or frozen for up to 3 months.

MAKES ABOUT 6 CUPS

Pasta

Pasta

Fresh Pasta Dough

Pici with Extra Virgin Olive Oil,
Toasted Bread Crumbs, Parmigiano-Reggiano,
and Cracked Black Pepper

Pumpkin Ravioli with Brown
Butter Sage and Pancetta Cracklings

Tagliatelle with Fresh
Fava Beans and Preserved Lemon Cream

Porcini Mushroom, Roasted
Chicken, and Walnut Cream "Fazzoletti"
Handkerchief Lasagna

Orecchiette with Sweet Vidalia
Onion, Cavolo Nero, Golden Raisins,
and Pine Nuts

Corzetti with Herbed Veal
and Sun-Dried Tomato Polpettine

FRESH PASTA DOUGH

*Although making fresh pasta might seem intimidating and
time consuming, it is actually quite easy. A large work-surface
area is the key to its preparation. The rewards of freshly
made pasta are well worth the effort.*

---

4 cups all-purpose flour, preferably an Italian "tipo 00" style

4 extra-large eggs

1 tablespoon BELLA CUCINA Extra Virgin Olive Oil

¾ teaspoon kosher salt

~

TO PREPARE BY HAND: Pour 3½ cups flour on
work surface and make a well in the center of the flour.
Crack the eggs, add the whites and the yolk to the well, and
add the oil and salt. Beat with a fork or use a whisking motion
with your hands to lightly mix together the eggs, oil,
and salt. Then gradually bring in the flour from all sides
until the mixture forms a smooth and pliable dough.
Form into a ball for kneading.

TO PREPARE IN A FOOD PROCESSOR: Place 3½ cups flour,
eggs, and salt in the processor bowl and pulse until the dough
just comes together. Dough should be crumbly and pliable. Remove
the dough to your work surface and shape it into a ball.

Whether working by hand or with a food processor,
now knead the dough 5 to 10 minutes by hand, adding flour
from the remaining ½ cup as needed if the dough seems
too sticky, until smooth and elastic.

Cover dough with an inverted bowl or in plastic wrap
and let rest 20 minutes before shaping. Allow the
dough to come to room temperature before rolling out.
The dough may be refrigerated up to 2 days.

Roll out using an electric or
hand-crank machine to desired thickness.

MAKES APPROXIMATELY 1 POUND PASTA

PICI WITH EXTRA VIRGIN OLIVE OIL, TOASTED BREADCRUMBS, PARMIGIANO-REGGIANO, AND CRACKED BLACK PEPPER

*Pici is a traditional hand-made pasta from Tuscany.
It is like spaghetti, but much thicker and with more "tooth" and texture
to the bite. If you cannot find pici at your specialty grocer, a
good durum spaghetti, such as that made by Martelli, will do nicely.
For this pasta, it's essential to use premium quality ingredients,
especially the extra virgin olive oil.*

*I prefer a fruity, green, and peppery oil, like our
Bella Cucina Extra Virgin Olive Oil, reminiscent of the types
found in small frantoios (olive pressing cooperatives)
in Tuscany. You may want to consider tossing the ingredients
at the table; every moment of this aromatic
experience is worth savoring.*

FOR THE TOASTED BREADCRUMBS:
1 loaf focaccia bread
¼ cup olive oil

❧

1 pound pici or other pasta
(choose a high-quality durum wheat pasta)

½ cup BELLA CUCINA Extra Virgin Olive Oil

¼ cup freshly grated Parmigiano-Reggiano

1 tablespoon freshly, coarsely cracked black pepper

❧

TO PREPARE THE TOASTED BREADCRUMBS:
Fresh breadcrumbs really enhance this recipe. To make them, cut a loaf
of focaccia bread into one-inch cubes, drizzle with olive oil, and
bake at 350°F for 12 to 15 minutes, rotating occasionally. Once cooled,
crush in a mortar and pestle, or pulse in a food processor.

In a large pot, bring 4 quarts of salted water to a boil.
Add the pasta and cook until al dente.

When cooked, drain and transfer to a large serving bowl.
Add the olive oil, bread crumbs, Parmigiano-Reggiano, and
pepper and toss until well coated.

SERVES 4 TO 6

This ravioli dish is perhaps
my favorite pasta. Whenever I'm in
Italy and see it on the menu,
I order it. The pasta is

{ *Light and Pillowy* }

and the flavors of the
pumpkin melt into the butter and
sage sauce. Delizioso!

PUMPKIN RAVIOLI with BROWN BUTTER SAGE and PANCETTA CRACKLINGS

*Fresh pasta sheets are now readily available in most
specialty food stores, so if you do not want to make your own pasta,
there is an easy alternative for enjoying this savory dish often.*

½ cup semolina

1 recipe pasta dough *(recipe, page 54)* or 1 pound
fresh pasta sheets from your local specialty food market

2 egg yolks, beaten

One 6-ounce jar BELLA CUCINA Sweet Pumpkin Pesto

1 ounce sliced pancetta

8 tablespoons *(1 stick)* unsalted butter

15 to 20 fresh sage leaves, long stems removed

Freshly grated Parmigiano-Reggiano

Spread the semolina evenly on a sheetpan and set aside.
On a lightly floured work surface, roll out pasta dough into thin
sheets. Once all the sheets are rolled out, take one and lay
it on the refloured surface; brush lightly with egg yolks. Beginning
1 to 1½ inches in from the near edge of the pasta, place a single
row of pumpkin pesto dollops *(1 tablespoon per dollop)* on
the pasta, spaced 3 inches apart. Gently fold the pasta over
the pesto dollops *(as shown at left)*; cut into squares with a knife or
pasta wheel, leaving a 1-inch edge of pasta around the filling
and gently pressing the edges together to remove any air bubbles.

If not using ravioli immediately, place in freezer.
When ravioli are frozen, transfer them to a plastic bag and keep flat.
They may be kept, frozen, up to one month. When ready
to cook frozen ravioli, do not defrost, but rather add them
directly from the freezer to boiling salted water.

When ready to prepare the dish, bring 4 quarts salted water
to a boil in a large pot. Brush the semolina off the ravioli and gently add
them to boiling water. Cook until al dente or until ravioli float
to the top, about 3 to 5 minutes depending on whether
ravioli are fresh or frozen. Drain and transfer to a serving bowl.

Place a medium sauté pan over medium heat. Add pancetta and cook,
stirring, until crisp, about 5 to 7 minutes. Remove pancetta from pan and let
drain on paper towels. When cool, break or chop pancetta into pieces.
Add butter to sauté pan and heat until foaming *(be careful not to burn the butter)*.
Add sage leaves and cook, stirring, until leaves are crisp and
the butter is nut brown in color. Remove pan from heat, stir in chopped
pancetta cracklings, and pour mixture over the cooked ravioli.

Sprinkle with Parmigiano-Reggiano and serve.

SERVES 4

TAGLIATELLE WITH FRESH FAVA BEANS AND PRESERVED LEMON CREAM

*Celebrate the fresh flavors of spring with this recipe,
which takes full advantage of the first fresh crop of fava beans and
the floral undertones of our unique Preserved Lemon Cream.
If fava beans are not available, use roasted asparagus
or fresh English peas instead.*

———— ✦ ————

1 pound fava beans, shelled

1 pound tagliatelle or other pasta
(choose a high-quality durum wheat pasta)

One 6-ounce jar BELLA CUCINA Preserved Lemon Cream

½ cup mascarpone cheese

⅓ cup BELLA CUCINA Extra Virgin Olive Oil

1 teaspoon kosher salt

⅛ teaspoon freshly cracked black pepper

Parmigiano-Reggiano shavings, for garnish

☙

In a large pot, bring 4 quarts salted water to a boil.
Add the shelled fava beans and cook until tender, about 2 minutes.
Ladle the beans out of the water and set aside until they
are cool enough to handle, then remove and discard their skins.

Add the pasta to the boiling water and cook until al dente.
Meanwhile, in a large bowl mix together the lemon
cream, mascarpone, oil, salt, and pepper until smooth. When
the pasta is cooked, drain and add to the bowl with the
lemon cream mixture. Toss with the fava beans and serve,
topped with Parmigiano-Reggiano shavings.

SERVES 4

There is nothing quite like the
earthy perfume of

Fresh porcini mushrooms

just foraged from the damp forest
after the first autumn rains.

❧

PORCINI MUSHROOM, ROASTED CHICKEN, AND WALNUT CREAM "FAZZOLETTI" HANDKERCHIEF LASAGNA

Fresh pasta makes this dish light and delicate.
The thin pasta sheets practically float on the plate.

½ cup chicken broth

¼ ounce dried porcini mushrooms (about 2 tablespoons)

One 6-ounce jar BELLA CUCINA Walnut Sage Pesto

2 ounces thinly sliced pancetta

1 tablespoon unsalted butter

½ pound fresh shitake mushrooms

1 tablespoon chopped fresh sage leaves

2 cups roasted chicken (*light or dark meat*)
torn into bite-sized pieces

1 recipe Fresh Pasta Dough (*recipe, page 54*) or
½ pound fresh pasta sheets from your local specialty food market

½ cup heavy cream

4 tablespoons chopped fresh Italian flat-leaf parsley

In a small saucepan, bring the broth and porcini mushrooms
to a boil. Remove from heat and let sit 15 minutes, so flavor can develop.
Strain through a triple-lined cheesecloth into a medium bowl and twist
the cheesecloth into a tight pouch to squeeze out any juices. Add the
walnut pesto to the porcini broth and stir until smooth. Discard porcini
mushrooms and set the pesto broth aside until ready to use.

Cut pancetta into ¼-inch pieces and cook in a sauté pan
over medium-high heat until crispy. Remove pancetta from
the pan with a slotted spoon and reserve for garnish.

Add the butter to the same saucepan. Increase heat to high, melt butter,
add shitake mushrooms and sage, and sauté until the mushrooms
are brown and caramelized. Remove mushrooms from pan and set aside.
Deglaze pan with ¼ cup pesto broth, scraping up the seared bits
from the bottom of the pan. Add the deglazing mixture to the remaining
pesto broth. Toss the shitake mushrooms with the roasted chicken
pieces and half of the pesto broth. Set aside until ready to use.

Cut the pasta into twelve 3-inch squares. Cook pasta sheets in boiling
salted water until al dente. Remove from the water with a slotted
spoon and transfer to a towel to drain. Cover to keep warm.

TO ASSEMBLE LASAGNA: Place one square of pasta on each plate and
evenly spread one-twelfth (*about 2 tablespoons*) of the chicken and mushroom
mixture on the pasta. Top with another sheet of pasta. Put the same amount of
filling on the second sheet, top with a third pasta layer, and finish with
a final 2-tablespoon dollop of chicken and mushroom mixture on top.

In a sauté pan, heat the cream over high heat until
reduced by half. Add the remaining pesto broth. Pour one-quarter
of the sauce over each plate of assembled lasagna.

Top with pancetta and parsley and serve immediately.

SERVES 4

ORRECHIETTE WITH SWEET VIDALIA ONION, CAVOLO NERO, GOLDEN RAISINS, AND PINE NUTS

A traditional Italian leafy green in the kale family, cavolo nero is slightly sweet yet bitter with a wonderfully meaty texture. We immediately fell in love with it when we first tried it in Tuscany. Cavolo nero goes by many different names in the United States, such as Tuscan kale, black cabbage, lacinata, and dinosaur kale. If you can't find it at your local farmer's market or specialty food store, substitute Swiss chard in this recipe.

---

1 pound orecchiete or other pasta
(*choose a high-quality durum wheat pasta*)

½ cup Madeira

1 cup golden raisins

¼ cup currants

¼ cup BELLA CUCINA Extra Virgin Olive Oil

2 cloves chopped fresh garlic

1 bunch chiffonade of cavolo nero or Swiss chard (*unless the leaves of the cavolo nero are as large as your hand, remove the stems before chopping*)

½ cup chicken or vegetable broth

One 6-ounce jar BELLA CUCINA Sweet Vidalia Onion Pesto

¼ cup toasted pine nuts

Kosher salt and freshly cracked black pepper to taste

Parmigiano-Reggiano shavings, for garnish

In a large pot, bring 4 quarts salted water to a boil. Add the pasta and cook until al dente. Meanwhile, in a small saucepan, bring the Madeira and ½ cup water to a boil. Stir in the raisins and currants. Remove the pan from heat and let sit until the fruit is plump, about 10 minutes. Set aside.

In a sauté pan, heat the olive oil over medium heat until hot but not smoking. Add the garlic and cook, stirring, for about 15 seconds. Discard garlic clove. Add the cavolo nero and cook, stirring, until wilted. Remove the pan from the heat.

When the pasta is cooked, drain and return it to the large pot. Add raisins and currants in their juices, cavolo nero, broth, onion pesto, and pine nuts and toss gently to combine. Season to taste. Serve immediately, topped with Parmigiano-Reggiano shavings.

SERVES 6

CORZETTI WITH HERBED VEAL AND SUN-DRIED TOMATO POLPETTINE

Polpette are the Italian meatballs found in many sizes and flavors. These are the smaller version—called polpettine—which are the perfect bite-sized pieces to savor with every mouthful of pasta. The polpettine can also be served as an appetizer with warm Farmhouse Sugo Pasta Sauce on the side for dipping.

½ pound fresh ground veal

½ pound fresh ground beef

¼ cup finely ground breadcrumbs
(use fresh breadcrumbs if possible, recipe page 56)

½ cup BELLA CUCINA Sun-Dried Tomato Pesto

1 large egg ✺ 1 tablespoon chopped fresh oregano

1 tablespoon chopped fresh Italian flat-leaf parsley

1 tablespoon chopped fresh basil, plus additional torn leaves for garnish

Kosher salt and freshly cracked black pepper to taste

¼ cup BELLA CUCINA Extra Virgin Olive Oil

1 jar BELLA CUCINA Farmhouse Sugo Pasta Sauce

1 pound corzetti *(see photos at right)* or your favorite high-quality durum wheat pasta, prepared according to package directions

Parmigiano-Reggiano shavings, for garnish

☙

Line a sheetpan with parchment paper. In a large mixing bowl, add the ground meats, breadcrumbs, sun-dried tomato pesto, egg, herbs, salt, and pepper. Mix together by hand until well incorporated. Roll into 1-inch balls *(approximately 30)* and place on the sheetpan until ready to use.

In a large nonstick skillet, heat the oil over medium heat until hot but not smoking. Add the polpettine in batches, being careful not to overcrowd the pan, and fry until cooked through and browned on all sides, shaking the pan periodically to prevent sticking, about 3 to 4 minutes. Add the sugo pasta sauce to the pan and cook until the sauce is warmed and the polpettine are thoroughly cooked. Pour over pasta and serve. Top with Parmigiano-Reggiano and fresh torn basil leaves.

SERVES 6

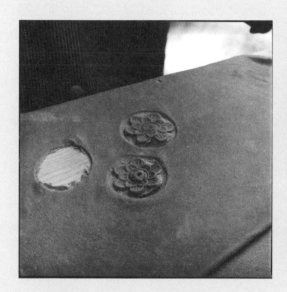

Made with a wooden stamp,
Corzetti is a delightfully fun presentation
of pasta from the

{ *Ligurian countryside.* }

Roll sheets of fresh pasta as thin as lasagna sheets,
press the stamp at the edges and turn slightly,
flipping up coins of pasta from the sheet.

❦

Piatti

{ Main Courses }

LEMON CAPER VEAL SCALOPPINE

MOROCCAN LAMB AND
EGGPLANT BAKED TOMATOES

ITALIAN SAUSAGE WITH FENNEL
AND ROASTED PEPPERS OVER POLENTA

OLIVADA AND ROSEMARY STUFFED
LEG OF LAMB

PANCETTA BRAISED RABBIT
WITH PRUNE PLUMS

ARTICHOKE LEMON AND CHICKEN STEW
WITH PINE NUT AND
PRESERVED LEMON COUSCOUS

CHICKEN BREASTS STUFFED WITH HERBED
GOAT CHEESE AND SUN-DRIED TOMATO PESTO

BRANZINI BAKED SEABASS WITH PRESERVED
LEMONS, OLIVES, AND SALSA VERDE

LITTLENECK CLAMS WITH
PRESERVED LEMON AND HERB BUTTER

EGGPLANT INVOLTINI

Macelleria

DEFT HANDS CUTTING WITH
SUCH PRECISION AND CARE. A LIFETIME
OF MASTERING THIS ART.

LEMON CAPER VEAL SCALOPPINE

This recipe is my standby when I need to cook something delicious and satisfying in a hurry. Because the dessert cream adds a nice lemon creaminess to the sauce, there is an unlikely surprise in this savory dish.

---

1 tablespoon BELLA CUCINA Extra Virgin Olive Oil

1 tablespoon unsalted butter

4 veal scaloppine

¼ cup chicken stock

½ cup white wine

1 tablespoon salted capers, rinsed

2 tablespoons BELLA CUCINA Preserved Lemon Cream

In a large sauté pan, heat the olive oil and butter over medium-high heat until smoking. Add the veal and cook on both sides until browned, about 2 minutes per side.

Remove the veal from the pan and set aside.
Add the chicken stock to the pan and cook, stirring and scraping up the bits of meat from the pan. Add the white wine and capers. Cook until sauce thickens, about 1 minute. Whisk in the preserved lemon cream. Return veal to the pan to warm and serve immediately.

SERVES 2

MOROCCAN LAMB AND
EGGPLANT BAKED TOMATOES

*This dish combines the flavors of the Mediterranean,
including our unique pearl pasta, otherwise
known as toasted couscous. I love this dish served
with sautéed fresh spinach leaves
tossed with freshly squeezed lemon juice.*

---

4 large vine-ripe tomatoes with stems

1 tablespoon BELLA CUCINA Extra Virgin Olive Oil

½ cup chopped onion

½ pound ground lamb

One 6-ounce jar BELLA CUCINA Roasted Eggplant Pesto

½ cup cooked BELLA CUCINA Pearl Pasta
(prepared according to package directions)

2 tablespoons toasted pine nuts

1 tablespoon golden raisins

1 teaspoon cumin

½ teaspoon kosher salt

⅛ teaspoon freshly cracked black pepper

1 teaspoon chopped fresh mint

PREHEAT OVEN TO 350°F.
Slice off the top of each tomato and reserve for garnish.
Using a spoon or melon baller, scoop out the
tomato seeds and flesh. Squeeze seeds through a strainer
and discard; chop tomato flesh. Set aside the
hollowed tomatoes and tops and the chopped flesh.

In a large sauté pan, heat the olive oil over medium-high
heat until hot but not smoking. Add the onion and cook,
stirring, until soft but not browned, 5 to 7 minutes.
Add the lamb and cook until browned, 10 minutes. Remove the
pan from heat. Add the reserved chopped tomato flesh,
eggplant pesto, pearl pasta, pine nuts, raisins, cumin, salt,
pepper, and mint and mix until well combined.
Fill the hollowed tomatoes with the lamb mixture.
Place the tops on each tomato and bake
until tomatoes are soft, 20 to 25 minutes.

Serve warm.

SERVES 4

ITALIAN SAUSAGE WITH FENNEL AND ROASTED PEPPERS OVER POLENTA

*This dish combines the traditional flavors of
Italian cuisine. In the summer, leave the sausages out of the
sauce and grill them, whole, over a hardwood fire.
The polenta can also be grilled by turning the cooked polenta
out on to a buttered sheetpan, letting it cool, slicing it into pieces
and brushing them with olive oil, and grilling them
until warm. Serve with sauce on the side.*

---

2 tablespoons BELLA CUCINA Extra Virgin Olive Oil

1 cup thinly sliced fresh fennel

1 cup thinly sliced yellow onion

1 cup sliced red pepper

1 cup sliced yellow pepper

4 Italian sausages, casings removed

One 6-ounce jar BELLA CUCINA Sweet Pepper Pesto

Thinly sliced fresh basil leaves, for garnish

FOR THE HERBED POLENTA:

1 tablespoon chopped fresh rosemary

1½ teaspoons kosher salt

1 cup polenta

1 cup freshly grated Parmigiano-Reggiano

1 tablespoon unsalted butter

In a medium sauté pan, heat the olive oil over medium heat.
Add the fennel, onion, and yellow and red peppers and cook, stirring,
until soft but not brown, about 15 minutes. Remove the vegetables
from the pan and set aside. Return the pan to medium heat,
add the sausages, and cook, breaking the meat into small pieces
with a wooden spoon, until thoroughly cooked, about 10 to 15 minutes.
Stir in the pepper mixture and the sweet pepper pesto. Keep warm.

TO PREPARE THE POLENTA: In a large saucepan, bring 4 cups
water to a boil. Reduce the heat to medium and stir in the
rosemary and salt. Slowly pour in the polenta. Whisk constantly
until it thickens, about 25 to 30 minutes. Add the
Parmigiano-Reggiano and butter and mix until combined.

*Serve the polenta immediately, topped with the
sausages and sweet peppers and garnished with basil.*

SERVES 6

74

OLIVADA AND ROSEMARY STUFFED
LEG OF LAMB

*Roasted in the oven or grilled over hardwood, this dish
is best made with tender spring lamb from the leg of the lamb, cut
into a small roast. Have your butcher trim and butterfly the roast
for you so it's ready to dress. This dish can be made quickly,
but it tastes like you spent hours in the kitchen.*

FOR THE STUFFING:

One 6-ounce jar BELLA CUCINA Olivada Olive Pesto

¼ lemon rind from a jar of BELLA CUCINA Preserved Lemons,
chopped *(rinse lemon and remove pulp and discard before chopping)*

1 tablespoon capers

1 tablespoon fresh squeezed lemon juice

2 tablespoons Italian flat-leaf parsley

Kosher salt and freshly cracked black pepper to taste

☙

One butterflied leg of lamb *(about 3 pounds)*

FOR THE SEA SALT CRUST:

1 tablespoon Maldon sea salt or coarsely ground sea salt

1 tablespoon fennel seeds

1 teaspoon freshly cracked black pepper

3 tablespoons BELLA CUCINA Extra Virgin Olive Oil

PREHEAT OVEN TO 375°F.
TO PREPARE THE STUFFING: In a small bowl, mix
together the olive pesto, preserved lemon, capers, lemon juice,
parsley, salt, and pepper until well combined.

Open up the butterflied lamb and evenly spread the pesto
mixture over one side of the meat. Close and skewer in several places
at the seam or tie the leg with butcher string to secure.

TO PREPARE THE SEA SALT CRUST: Combine the salt, fennel
seeds, and pepper. Rub the outside of the lamb with oil and coat with
the salt mixture. Marinate, refrigerated, at least an hour or overnight.

Roast until pink and tender, about 1 hour, until an instant-read
thermometer inserted into the thickest part of the meat reads 130° to
135°F *(the temperature will rise about 5 degrees once out of the oven).*

*Let rest 10 to 15 minutes before carving.
Pour pan drippings over the meat; serve hot.*

SERVES 8

PANCETTA BRAISED RABBIT
WITH PRUNE PLUMS

*This dish combines both sweet and sour flavors, traditionally
known as agridolce in Tuscan cooking. If the vinegar is too tart for your
palate, simply cut back on the quantity until it suits your taste.
Rabbit can be difficult to find, so you may want to ask your local
butcher to special order it for you. Otherwise, free-range
chicken or guinea hens are delicious alternatives.*

I whole rabbit cut into 6 to 8 pieces

2 cups all-purpose flour

I tablespoon kosher salt

I teaspoon freshly cracked black pepper

2 tablespoons chopped fresh sage leaves

¼ pound sliced pancetta

2 tablespoons BELLA CUCINA Extra Virgin Olive Oil

2 tablespoons unsalted butter

I pound Italian prune plums or fresh apricots
(or any other fresh stone fruit in season, pitted and halved)

2 cups red wine vinegar

I cup Vin Santo ❁ ½ cup sugar

I cup BELLA CUCINA Sweet Vidalia Onion Pesto

2 cups chicken broth

❦

PREHEAT OVEN TO 350°F.
Combine flour, salt, and pepper. Add the sage and mix
well to combine. Transfer the flour to a plate.

Wrap each piece of rabbit with two slices of pancetta, allowing the pancetta
to overlap slightly so it sticks. Dredge each piece of rabbit in the flour mixture and
shake off the excess. Set the rabbit pieces aside and discard the flour.

In a medium skillet, heat the olive oil and butter over medium-high heat
until the butter is foaming. Add the rabbit one piece at a time without crowding
the pan and sauté until golden brown, about 3 minutes per side. As they
are browned, transfer the rabbit pieces to an ovenproof casserole and set aside.

In a blender or food processor, process 6 plum halves
with the red wine vinegar until smooth. Set aside.

When all of the rabbit is cooked, add the Vin Santo and sugar to the pan and
cook over medium-high heat, stirring and scraping up the brown bits. When the
sugar has dissolved, add the plum purée and simmer over medium heat
until the liquid reduces by half. Stir in the onion pesto and chicken broth.

Meanwhile, layer the remaining plum halves together with the
browned rabbit pieces in the casserole. Pour the plum purée over the
rabbit and plums. Bake until the rabbit is tender and the plums
are soft but still retain some texture, about 45 minutes.

SERVES 6

ARTICHOKE LEMON AND CHICKEN STEW
WITH PINE NUT AND
PRESERVED LEMON COUSCOUS

*This dish is also delicious with boned pieces of lamb shoulder
instead of chicken. The braising allows for the chicken
to become so tender that it falls off the bone.*

⅓ cup BELLA CUCINA Extra Virgin Olive Oil

8 skinless bone-in chicken thighs

1 onion, chopped

1 cup chopped carrots

2 large garlic cloves, chopped

1 tablespoon chopped fresh rosemary

One 6-ounce jar BELLA CUCINA Artichoke Lemon Pesto

4 cups chicken stock

1 teaspoon fresh thyme leaves

¼ cup chopped fresh Italian flat-leaf parsley

Kosher salt and freshly cracked black pepper to taste

FOR THE PINE NUT AND PRESERVED LEMON COUSCOUS:

1 cup BELLA CUCINA Pearl Pasta

¼ cup toasted pine nuts

2 tablespoons chopped BELLA CUCINA Preserved Lemon rind
(rinse lemon and remove and discard pulp before chopping)

2 tablespoons BELLA CUCINA Extra Virgin Olive Oil

1 tablespoon BELLA CUCINA Preserved Lemon Cream

In a large, heavy sauté pan with a tight-fitting lid, heat 3 tablespoons
of olive oil over medium-high heat until hot but not smoking. Add the
chicken thighs and cook on both sides until well browned, 3 to 4 minutes.
As they are browned, transfer the chicken thighs to a plate and set aside.

When all of the chicken is browned, add the remaining oil to the pan.
Add the onion, carrots, garlic, and rosemary; cook, stirring, until soft,
about 10 minutes. Stir in the artichoke lemon pesto, stock, thyme,
parsley, salt, and pepper. Bring to a gentle simmer, stirring and scraping up
the browned bits in the pan. Add the chicken, cover, and simmer over
low heat for about 1½ hours, until the meat is tender.

TO PREPARE THE PINE NUT AND PRESERVED LEMON COUSCOUS:
Cook the pearl pasta according to package directions.
Once pearl pasta is cooked, add the pine nuts, preserved lemon,
olive oil, and lemon cream and gently stir until combined.

Serve the chicken over couscous.

SERVES 4

CHICKEN BREASTS STUFFED WITH HERBED GOAT CHEESE AND SUN-DRIED TOMATO PESTO

This simple dish combines two of everyone's favorite flavors, sun-dried tomatoes and basil. The recipe calls for serving this dish as a main course, but it has always been a favorite of mine as an appetizer when cut into pinwheels and served with the sauce for dipping.

———◆—◆———

4 boneless, skinless chicken breast halves (about 1½ pounds)

8 ounces soft goat cheese, at room temperature

2 tablespoons BELLA CUCINA Sun-Dried Tomato Pesto

2 large cloves garlic, chopped

4 tablespoons BELLA CUCINA Fresh Basil Pesto

¼ cup breadcrumbs

2 tablespoons BELLA CUCINA Extra Virgin Olive Oil

1½ cups BELLA CUCINA Farmhouse Sugo Pasta Sauce

Kosher salt and freshly cracked black pepper to taste

☙

PREHEAT OVEN TO 375°F.
Place the chicken breasts, one at a time, between two sheets of
waxed paper or plastic wrap. Gently pound each breast with the flat side
of a meat cleaver or a mallet to thickness of ½ inch. Set aside.

In a small mixing bowl combine the goat cheese, sun-dried tomato
pesto, and garlic. Mix until thoroughly combined and smooth.

Divide the goat cheese mixture among the chicken breasts,
and with a spatula spread the cheese evenly from end to end. At one
narrow end of each chicken breast, place 1 tablespoon basil pesto.
Starting at that end, tightly roll up each chicken breast to form a log.
*(This portion may be prepared up to 2 days ahead of time. Wrap each piece
tightly in plastic and refrigerate until ready to use.)*

Place the chicken on a parchment-lined sheetpan.
Pat the breadcrumbs on top of each piece and drizzle with oil.
Bake until cooked through but still tender, 20 to 30 minutes.
Meanwhile heat the pasta sauce. When the chicken is done,
spoon the warmed sauce on to individual plates or on
to a platter, then place the chicken on top.
(Alternatively, you can serve the chicken sliced, cut on the bias).

SERVES 4

Branzini Baked Sea Bass with Preserved Lemons, Olives, and Salsa Verde

*I like to bake this dish in a terra cotta planter base
(one without a hole in the bottom) and serve it at
the table straight from the oven.*

———— ·◆· ————

4 sea bass or halibut fillets, about 6 ounces each

¼ cup sliced BELLA CUCINA Preserved Lemons
(rinse lemon and remove and discard pulp before slicing)

½ cup BELLA CUCINA Antipasti Olives

3 tablespoons BELLA CUCINA Sicilian Lemon Aromatic Oil

Kosher salt and freshly cracked black pepper to taste

PREHEAT OVEN TO 375°F.
Cut fillets into 2-inch pieces and place in an ovenproof baking dish
or terra-cotta platter. Scatter the preserved lemon slices and olives over
fillets. Drizzle with lemon oil and season with salt and pepper. Bake
until the fish is just cooked *(it should be firm to the touch)*, 7 to 10 minutes.

Serve with Salsa Verde (recipe below).

SERVES 4

Salsa Verde

½ cup parsley leaves

2 tablespoons plus 1 teaspoon champagne vinegar

Zest and juice of one lemon

2 tablespoons chopped fresh chives

2 tablespoons capers, drained

2 large cloves garlic, chopped

1 teaspoon coarsely chopped sage leaves

1 teaspoon fresh oregano leaves

1 teaspoon kosher salt

1 teaspoon freshly cracked black pepper

¾ cup BELLA CUCINA Extra Virgin Olive Oil

2 tablespoons BELLA CUCINA Sicilian Lemon Aromatic Oil

᪣

In a blender or food processor, add all of the ingredients
except the oils. Process on high speed, slowly adding
the olive and lemon oils in a steady stream through the top
of the blender or food processor, until the mixture
is smooth and emulsified.

MAKES ½ CUP

LITTLENECK CLAMS WITH PRESERVED LEMON AND HERB BUTTER

Any fresh shellfish can be used here with delicious results.
This easy-to-prepare, light dish can also be served over linguine.

———

3 pounds littleneck clams
1 tablespoon BELLA CUCINA Extra Virgin Olive Oil
1 tablespoon chopped shallots
¼ cup white wine
4 tablespoons Preserved Lemon and Herb Butter *(recipe below)*
Chopped fresh chives, for garnish

Rinse the clams to remove all the sediment from the shells,
scrubbing with a brush if very gritty. Discard any shellfish that have
already opened and those with broken shells.

In a large saucepan with a tight-fitting lid, heat the olive oil over
medium heat and cook the shallots, stirring, until soft and translucent.
Add the white wine and cook an additional minute to remove the alcohol flavor.
Add the clams and cover the pan. Cook until the clams have opened,
3 to 4 minutes, stirring or shaking the pan occasionally to distribute heat
evenly in the pan. Remove pan from heat and spoon the clams
and their juice into four dishes. Top each serving with 1 tablespoon
Preserved Lemon and Herb Butter and garnish with chives.

SERVES 4

PRESERVED LEMON AND HERB BUTTER

8 tablespoons unsalted butter, softened
2 tablespoons BELLA CUCINA Preserved Lemons, chopped
(rinse lemon and remove pulp before chopping)
1 tablespoon fresh chives, chopped

Combine all ingredients, folding gently until well incorporated.
On parchment paper, form butter mixture into a sausage-like
form and roll up tightly. Press sides flat and twist ends of paper like
a candy wrapper. Refrigerate up to 1 week until needed.

TO USE: Unroll the parchment paper and cut butter into slices.
Use on pan-seared fish, grilled steaks and chicken, fresh shellfish, or pasta
as a quick condiment or sauce. Keep leftovers in the freezer for
quick meals. Simply remove from freezer and let soften 10 to 15 minutes.
The butter will continue to melt when it hits the hot food.

MAKES 8 SERVINGS

Eggplant Involtini

In Italian, involtini means stuffed and rolled and usually involves pasta. This dish is unique in that the cannelloni are made instead with grilled strips of eggplant. It makes a light, vegetarian lunch or dinner that can be prepared ahead of time and baked just before serving.

———✦———

1 large eggplant, cut lengthwise into ½-inch strips
⅓ cup BELLA CUCINA Extra Virgin Olive Oil
Kosher salt and freshly cracked black pepper to taste

FOR THE FILLING:
¾ cup ricotta cheese
¼ cup Parmigiano-Reggiano
½ cup BELLA CUCINA Roasted Eggplant Pesto
1 whole egg
2 tablespoons torn fresh basil leaves
1 teaspoon chopped fresh mint leaves
½ teaspoon kosher salt
¼ teaspoon freshly cracked black pepper
2 cups BELLA CUCINA Organic Passata al Pomodoro
8 ounces fresh mozzarella
Torn fresh basil leaves, for garnish
Freshly grated Parmigiano-Reggiano, for garnish

❧

Drizzle the eggplant slices with the olive oil;
sprinkle with salt and pepper.

Prepare a medium-hot grill or heat a grill pan over medium heat;
grill eggplant slices until light brown on both sides, about 1 minute
per side. (*Alternatively, you can sauté the eggplant. In this case, do not
drizzle slices with olive oil; instead, heat the oil in a sauté pan over medium heat
until hot but not smoking. Cook eggplant slices in oil until light brown on
both sides, about 2 minutes per side.*) Set eggplant strips aside.

TO PREPARE THE FILLING: In a medium mixing bowl
combine ricotta, Parmigiano-Reggiano, eggplant pesto, egg,
basil, mint, salt, and pepper; mix until well combined.

PREHEAT THE OVEN TO 350°F.
Pour the passata into a medium-sized ovenproof casserole.

Place 2 tablespoons of filling mixture at one narrow end
of an eggplant slice; loosely roll up the slice. Place the roll seam-side
down in casserole. Continue with remaining slices of eggplant.

Place one slice of mozzarella over each eggplant roll; bake until cheese
is melted, slightly brown, and bubbly, about 25 minutes.

Garnish with basil and Parmigiano-Reggiano and serve.

SERVES 4

Dolci

Sweets

CARAMEL POACHED PEARS

APRICOT BROWN BUTTER CROSTATA

CHOCOLATE ORANGE WALNUT TARTLETS

NOCCIOLA TIRAMISU

BUTTERMILK PANNA COTTA WITH
BLOOD ORANGE COMPOTE

FRESH BERRY PANETTONE

LEMON AND MINT GRANITA

LIMONCELLO

NOCINO

Caramel Poached Pears

*An elegant dessert that features this simple fall fruit,
you can try a variety of pears, such as seckel, Bartlett, or d'anjou,
for different flavors and textures. Whatever variety you choose,
the caramel is sure to make it molto bene!*

———————

4 ripe Comice or Bartlett pears or
8 miniature Seckel pears

¾ cup white wine

¼ cup Vin Santo

½ cup sugar

1 vanilla bean, cut in half lengthwise

½ cup Bella Cucina Dolci di Latte

❧

Using a vegetable peeler or paring knife, peel the pears,
keeping their stems attached. Remove the core from each pear
with a paring knife, cutting straight up from the bottom and
maintaining the core's cylindrical shape.

In a large saucepan, heat the wines, 1 cup water, sugar,
and vanilla bean over medium heat until the sugar dissolves.
Add the pears and simmer, uncovered, until they
can be easily pierced with a sharp knife.
Remove the pears with a slotted spoon and set aside.

Bring the remaining syrup to a boil and cook until reduced
to about ½ cup. Fold in the dolci di latte. You may serve this warm
or at room temperature. When ready to serve, pour ¼ cup
of the sauce on each of 4 plates and place a pear on top of each.
Pour the remaining sauce over pears and serve.

Serves 4

APRICOT BROWN BUTTER CROSTATA

*The nutty flavor from the browned butter is the key
ingredient in this traditional tart with a baked fresh fruit filling.
Pears, berries, and apples are all seasonal alternatives to
apricots in this fresh-fruit crostata. If you use a fruit other
than apricots, experiment with the various Bella Cucina
marmellatas to complement the flavor of the fruit.*

FOR THE DOUGH:

1½ cups all-purpose flour

¾ cup powdered sugar

1 tablespoon chopped Bella Cucina Preserved Lemons
(rinse lemon and remove and discard pulp before chopping)

Pinch kosher salt

12 tablespoons (1½ sticks) cold unsalted butter, cut into cubes

FOR THE FILLING:

8 tablespoons unsalted butter

3 eggs ❋ ¾ cup sugar

3 tablespoons all-purpose flour

2 tablespoons Bella Cucina Lemon Pear Limoncello Marmellata

1 teaspoon Vin Santo

1 teaspoon pure vanilla extract

10 to 12 fresh apricots, cut in half and pitted

TO PREPARE THE DOUGH: In a food processor or stand mixer,
process the flour, powdered sugar, lemons and salt until combined. Add the
butter and process until the dough just comes together. Remove from
the bowl and knead on a lightly floured surface just until the dough is smooth.
Cover in plastic wrap until ready to bake. Keeps up to three days
in the refrigerator and one month in the freezer.

PREHEAT OVEN TO 375°F.
Press the dough into a 9-inch tart pan with a removable bottom.
Chill dough 15 minutes. Prick the base of tart shell all over with a fork,
line with parchment paper, and place pie weights or dried beans
atop the parchment *(alternatively, this tart bakes beautifully without the weights)*.
Bake until light golden, 10 to 12 minutes. Remove parchment
paper and pie weights if using them and let tart cool.

TO PREPARE THE FILLING AND FINISH THE TART:
Keep oven at 375°F. In a small saucepan over low heat, cook butter until
it is nut brown. Transfer immediately to a bowl and let cool. Using a food processor,
combine eggs and sugar until thick and light in color. Add flour and cooled butter.
Lightly process in lemon pear marmellata, Vin Santo, and vanilla extract.

Arrange apricots cut-side up in the baked tart shell and pour the
custard filling over them. Bake until golden brown and a toothpick
inserted in the center comes out clean, 40 to 50 minutes.

SERVES 8

CHOCOLATE ORANGE WALNUT TARTLETS

The sweetness of the orange is a nice balance to the rich,
chocolaty flavor of this dessert tart. The velvety texture will melt in
your mouth. A perfect make-ahead dessert.

FOR THE TART DOUGH:

1½ cups all-purpose flour

¾ cup powdered sugar

Pinch kosher salt

12 tablespoons cold unsalted butter, cut into cubes

FOR THE FILLING:

One 6-ounce jar BELLA CUCINA Dolci Nocciola

4 eggs

½ cup sugar

2 tablespoons syrup from BELLA CUCINA Preserved Oranges

1 tablespoon BELLA CUCINA Mediterranean Tangerine Aromatic Oil

½ cup toasted walnut pieces

¼ cup coarsely chopped BELLA CUCINA Preserved Oranges
or ¼ cup BELLA CUCINA Blood Orange Marmellata

Powdered sugar for dusting

TO PREPARE THE DOUGH: In a food processor or stand mixer,
process the flour, powdered sugar, and salt until combined. Add the butter
and process until the dough just comes together. Remove from the
bowl and put together into a bowl. Cover in plastic wrap until ready to bake.
Keeps up to three days in the refrigerator and one month in the freezer.

PREHEAT OVEN TO 375°F.
Press the dough into six 4-inch tartlet pans with removable bottoms.
Chill for 15 minutes. Prick the bases of the tartlet shells and line with parchment
paper, adding pie weights or dried beans on top. Bake until lightly golden,
10 to 12 minutes. Remove parchment paper and pie weights and let cool.

PREPARE THE FILLING AND FINISH THE TARTLETS:
Keep oven at 375°F. In a large bowl, whisk together the dolci nocciola,
eggs, sugar, preserved orange syrup, and tangerine oil until smooth.
Fold in walnuts and preserved oranges or marmellata.

Pour mixture into baked tartlet shells and bake until a
toothpick inserted in the center of the tartlets comes out clean and
the chocolate is puffed around the edges, 20 to 25 minutes.

Dust the edges of the tartlets with powdered sugar before serving.

SERVES 6

NOCCIOLA TIRAMISU

*You will need twelve 5-ounce serving cups for this recipe,
preferably made of clear glass so your guests can see the layers.
(Alternatively, you can use one 8-by-8-inch baking dish.)
Once the serving cups or baking dish is filled with tiramisu, refrigerate
the dessert until it gets cold. For the best flavor, allow
tiramisu to chill 8 hours or up to 2 days.*

---

24 savoyardi or ladyfingers

9 tablespoons sugar

3 cups warm brewed coffee or espresso

1 tablespoon dark rum or Vin Santo

1 pound mascarpone

4 egg yolks

¼ cup BELLA CUCINA Dolci Nocciola

1 cup heavy cream

Shaved chocolate for garnish

8 chocolate-covered coffee beans, for garnish

Cut the savoyardi in half crosswise and set aside. In a
medium bowl, dissolve 3 tablespoons of the sugar in the warm coffee.
Add the Vin Santo and mix until well combined. Set aside.

Using an electric mixer with the paddle attachment,
blend the remaining sugar with the mascarpone, egg yolks,
and dolci nocciola until smooth and creamy.

TO ASSEMBLE THE TIRAMISU: Have ready twelve 5-ounce
serving cups or an 8-by-8-inch baking pan. Dip two halves of
savoyardi quickly in the coffee and place in the bottom of a cup or,
alternatively, two rows in the baking dish. Press down lightly and repeat
with the remaining cups. Top each cup with 2 tablespoons of the
mascarpone mixture, or spread half of the mixture in a thin layer
if using one pan. Once again dip two halves of savoyardi in the coffee for
each cup and place on top of the mascarpone layer. Press down lightly.

Replace the paddle attachment in the electric mixer with the whisk
attachment. Whip the cream into the remaining mascarpone mixture
until light and fluffy. Top each cup with 2 tablespoons of this
mixture, or add the remaining mixture if using one dish. Top with
chocolate shavings and garnish with chocolate-covered coffee beans.

Cover and refrigerate until ready to serve, preferably at
least 8 hours. Will keep covered in the refrigerator up to two days.

MAKES 12 INDIVIDUAL SERVINGS
OR 8 SERVINGS IN A SINGLE BAKING DISH

As Maria Callas sings to me
so passionately

I await the day and
ease myself awake.

Pen and paper my early morning confidant,
nonjudgmental of the scribblings of my thoughts.
In the end, there really could be nothing
more important than being right here, nowhere,
without an agenda. Riposo.

⚮

BUTTERMILK PANNA COTTA WITH
BLOOD ORANGE COMPOTE

*This is a wonderful dessert to make when you don't have
the time to cook but want to make a great impression. The silky texture
of the panna cotta adds an elegant finish to any meal.*

I envelope gelatin ✽ 2 ½ cups heavy cream

2 cups buttermilk ✽ I cup sugar

I tablespoon pure vanilla extract

I tablespoon almond or vegetable oil for coating cups

FOR THE COMPOTE:

I cup BELLA CUCINA Blood Orange Marmellata

½ cup fresh squeezed orange juice or blood orange juice

I teaspoon fresh lemon juice

෬

In a small bowl, sprinkle gelatin over ¼ cup cold water
until dissolved. Let stand for at least 3 minutes.

In a medium saucepan, heat cream, buttermilk, and sugar until
warm and sugar is dissolved. Remove from heat and cool slightly.
Whisk in dissolved gelatin and vanilla extract until smooth.

Brush eight shallow, wide 6-ounce plastic or glass cups
lightly with oil and fill half-way with panna cotta mixture.
Place in refrigerator until set, about 3 to 4 hours.

TO MAKE THE COMPOTE: In a large bowl, mix together
Blood Orange Marmellata, orange juice, and lemon juice until
well incorporated. Turn out panna cotta on to dessert plates
or shallow bowls and spoon compote over plates.

*In colder months, it's nice to serve the compote slightly warm.
Simply heat compote in the saucepan until warm to the touch and serve.*

SERVES 6

FRESH BERRY PANETTONE

*This is a delicious way to use leftover bread for a
sumptuous sweet dessert. A few simple ingredients from the pantry and
any fresh seasonal fruit make this recipe a year-round favorite.*

FOR THE BREAD PUDDING:

2 cups panettone or challah bread cut or torn into 1-inch pieces

1 cup mixed berries (*use any fresh fruit in season, or frozen*)

1½ cups heavy cream

½ cup BELLA CUCINA Preserved Lemon Cream

2 eggs

1 teaspoon pure vanilla extra

FOR THE TOPPING:

1½ cups heavy cream

½ cup BELLA CUCINA Preserved Lemon Cream

TO PREPARE THE BREAD PUDDING:
PREHEAT THE OVEN TO 375°F. In an overproof 9-by-12-inch
baking dish, layer the panettone and fresh fruit. In a large bowl,
whisk together the cream, preserved lemon cream, eggs,
and vanilla. Pour custard over the bread and berries to cover.
Bake until golden and bubbly around the edges, 40 to 50 minutes.

TO PREPARE THE TOPPING: Beat the
heavy cream with an electric mixer until whipped,
then fold in the preserved lemon cream.

Serve warm topped with the whipped lemon cream.

SERVES 6 TO 8

LEMON AND MINT GRANITA

*This refreshing Italian ice can be served between courses to
refresh the palate, for dessert, or in my favorite way, served on a sunny
weekend afternoon with a glass of Limoncello. Dolci far niente!*

---

1 ¼ cup sugar

1 cup freshly squeezed lemon juice

¼ cup Limoncello *(recipe, page 101)*, optional

¼ cup chopped BELLA CUCINA Preserved Lemons
(rinse lemons and remove and discard pulp before chopping)

1 tablespoon chopped fresh mint leaves

❦

TO PREPARE A SIMPLE SYRUP: In a small saucepan,
combine ¾ cup sugar and 1¼ cup water over medium heat and
cook until the sugar is dissolved. Immediately transfer the
syrup to a bowl and chill until ready to use.

Combine the syrup with all of the remaining ingredients
and place in a shallow glass dish. Chill in the freezer 6 to 8 hours
or overnight. When ready to serve, chill 6 glasses in the freezer
just until frosted. Place remaining ½ cup sugar on a small plate
and invert, one at a time, each glass and press it gently in the
sugar. Scrape the granita with a fork to form crystals
and serve in the garnished glasses.

SERVES 6

LIMONCELLO

*This is my version of this delicious, refreshing Sicilian drink to
serve as an aperitif with sparkling soda or straight-up as a dessert liqueur.
I also love to add it to desserts, like my Lemon Mint Granita
(recipe, page 98), as a flavorful ingredient.*

———— >·< ————

12 Meyer lemons *(use any other type of lemon if
Meyer Lemons are not available)*

2 sprigs lemon geranium or lemon verbena

One 750-milliliter bottle of high-quality vodka

FOR THE SIMPLE SYRUP:
2 cups sugar

Wash the lemons, removing any waxy residue. *(I sometimes place
lemons in boiling water for 2 to 3 minutes to help remove any stubborn wax.)*

With a vegetable peeler, remove the lemon peels,
being careful not to remove the white pith, since the pith will
add an unpleasant bitterness to the drink.

Place the lemon peels and lemon verbena leaves in a sterilized
two-quart glass jar. Pour the vodka over the lemon peel and leaves and seal.
Date the top of the jar. Store in a cool, dark place for 40 days.
Strain the vodka mixture into another sterilized jar and discard lemon peel
and leaves. The vodka mixture should have turned a beautiful yellow hue.

TO PREPARE THE SIMPLE SYRUP: In a saucepan, heat sugar
and 3 cups water until sugar is dissolved. Let cool. Add the sugar syrup
mixture to the vodka and seal jar. Date top of jar. Store an additional
40 days in a cool, dark place to develop and marry the flavors of limoncello.
Keep at room temperature or in freezer until ready to enjoy.

MAKES 2 QUARTS

———————————————

NOCINO

3 pounds green walnuts (about 20)

1 stick cinnamon ✺ 2 cloves

Two 750-milliliter bottles of high-quality vodka

2 cups sugar ✺ 1 star anise

One 750-milliliter bottle sangiovese or
dolcetto d'alba red wine

❦

Scrub the walnuts clean and place them in a sterilized
two-and-a-half quart jar. Add the cinnamon, cloves, and anise and
pour in the vodka. Let sit about 3 months *(be sure to date the top of the jar).*
The liquid will turn brown and the sediment will fall to the
bottom of the jar. When ready, strain through several layers of
cheesecloth until the liquid is clear. Discard spices.

In a saucepan, heat the sugar and 1 cup water until the
sugar is dissolved. Remove from heat and cool. Add sugar syrup
and wine to the walnut vodka. Let sit another month until
the flavors marry and the vodka mellows.

Serve at the holidays.
MAKES ABOUT 2 QUARTS

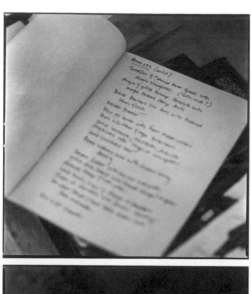

Riposa

Doors closed, lights out. Chiuso.
The silence of the city echoes through the narrow
cobblestone streets.

*It is afternoon
in Italy.*

A time for rest and rejuvenation
of the spirit and the appetite.

☙

TOSCANA

Verdant hills of every
imaginable hue undulate under the
caress of the summer sun.
Vines blossom after their winter sleep,
clinging to the embrace of the parched
earth below. Promises of a
harvest not so far away bring thoughts of
celebration of food and life.
Afternoon sun deceives us in its brilliance
as the wind rustles the cypress into a
slumbering lullaby for the siesta.
Clouds of white
cotton dance in playful laughter,
falling gracefully
from the trees wherever
the breeze decides.

GRAZIE

Gratitude

It's nearly impossible to begin to thank everyone who has educated, nurtured, and supported me on my way to writing this book.

I have been entrusted by former employers to use my creativity and pushed by colleagues to realize my talents, even when I thought I had exhausted all possibilities.

My thanks and appreciation to employees present and past who have supported my vision and contributed to this artisanal food company. Please accept my thanks for allowing and encouraging me to follow my passion and develop the foods I love.

MILLE GRAZIE to the many people who have helped in some way on this delicious journey.

A special thanks to *Paul Ferrari*, who first introduced me to the authentic Italy and inspired me to discover its treasures.

Thanks to *Joanne Weir*, my first and forever mentor, for your kind words and friendship.

To *Jennifer Peake*, who always had a smile and a fun story to keep us encouraged to stay on schedule.

To *Katja Burkett* and *Pamela Zuccker* whose tireless energy and wonderful designs help realize our vision beautifully.

To *Rob Brinson*, through whose lens we get an artistic view of who we are and what we do.

To *Louise Fili*, for her exquisite designs and bringing Italian elegance to BELLA CUCINA ARTFUL FOOD.

Thanks to friends and family, who never cease to amaze me with their support, encouragement, and love. Your understanding and patience is my wellspring.

Finally, a Dio (*my heavenly angel*), without whom none of this would be possible. I am merely an appreciative recipient of this beautiful gift of loving food which I am entrusted to share with others.

For *Smith*, whose partnership and creativity continue to inspire me to live LA BELLA VITA.

The small hilltown was love at first sight.
This hidden jewel might be missed as one
travels the Tuscan countryside.

Ancient healing waters flow from the hills,
nurturing the locals and rejuvenating the souls
of those passing through this small yet sophisticated
town where Silvestro and Daniela welcome you to
their ristorante and caffé where the locals
gather each morning to chat about the day.

Ciao to Marco and Alessandro who offered us
some fun and an evening in the vineyard.

And Loretta, who showed us her way to
make the perfect pasta, proudly sharing her
version of a thousand years of history and
tradition of Tuscan food.

Mille Grazie to the generous townspeople
who offered their "buon giorno" each morning
as they peered from their window terraces,
shutters opened to the day.

I look forward to my next visit with our
new friends and share a few more days living
"LA BELLA VITA" in Tuscany.

*Carved out of the hillside, San Casciano dei Bagni opens
its arms in an abraccio to all those willing to enter its path.*

RACCONTO
Our Story

With a passion for living artfully, BELLA CUCINA ARTFUL FOOD
celebrates artisan foods with our award-winning selection of
hand made, beautifully packaged culinary delights.
BELLA CUCINA celebrates the senses by continuing the tradition
of bringing food from the earth to the table.

*...so everyday you might share
with those you love your passion for
eating deliciously well.*

If you've been to Italy, even if only once, you probably understand my long-standing love affair with this simple yet elegant place—an organic country with intimate towns nestled in the never-ending landscape of cypress trees, or hidden between the knolls of centuries-old hills. A country filled with people passionate about life, food, wine, and conversation.

In Italy, people work to live, as they and their ancestors have always done. The artisan baker still tends to his hearth daily, the barista still pulls your morning espresso, the food markets still burst with the season's best offerings, and the local piazza still welcomes all who take a moment to pass through or stop for an idle chat.

With a passion for continuing those artisan traditions, Bella Cucina Artful Food was created as a celebration of Italian flavors, food and people. We make in our kitchens a pantry of projects based loosely on Mediterranean culinary traditions, reinterpreted in our own fresh style. Herein, we share a listing of our artisanal of foods.

BUON APPETITO!

PESTOS

Our nine pestos, each with its own distinct flavor profile, have enjoyed widespread success for their bright, fresh flavors and versatility. Use these ready-to-eat pestos in pasta dishes (like lasagne), antipasti (such as bruschetta), or swirled into sauces to enhance overall flavor.

Artichoke Lemon Pesto is simply our most popular flavor combination of artichoke hearts, freshly squeezed lemon, and extra-virgin olive oil.

Fresh Basil Pesto tastes like summer with its fragrant hand-picked leaves, imported Parmesan cheese and walnuts.

Sun-Dried Tomato Pesto is made from California's best vine-ripened sun-dried tomatoes. We add garlic, spices, and pine nuts for extra flavor.

Olivada Olive Pesto is pure Kalamata Olive flavor with a hint of fresh lemon and garlic.

Sweet Pepper Pesto features fire-roasted red peppers for a sweet, not hot, savory sauce. Pine nuts and extra-virgin olive oil give it a rich, concentrated flavor.

Roasted Eggplant Pesto is the best ripe eggplant, fresh garlic, and onion slowly roasted, together with a hint of cumin.

Walnut Sage Pesto combines sautéed garden sage leaves, fresh walnut halves, and imported Parmesan cheese. It makes a wonderful potato gratin.

Pumpkin Pesto is a savory combination of pumpkin, roasted onions, and imported Parmesan cheese. Use as a ravioli filling or risotto flavoring.

Sweet Vidalia Onion Pesto is made with Georgia-grown fresh-roasted Vidalia onions, garlic, and imported Parmesan cheese. Use this unique sauce as a base for pizzetta or toss with currants and pine nuts for an easy topping for penne pasta.

OLIVES

Marinated in a garlic-scented extra virgin olive oil blend, we mix six Italian-grown olive varieties and bottle them in two distinctly different ways: *Classic Antipasti Olives* are packed in old-fashioned Italian canning jars with metal closures and gasket lids (pictured above, at right). *Farmhouse Olives* feature the same wonderful olives in a screw-top lid and hand wrapped paper enclosure. Serve with a cheese selection from your local cheesemonger and your favorite red wine.

OILS AND VINEGAR

Extra-Virgin Olive Oil is cold-pressed in the classic Italian tradition. Only the finest tree-ripened California Mission olives are used, harvested and pressed at the early harvest in the fall each year. The resulting oil is an intense peppery and fruity oil, rich in texture and lively in color.

Cabernet Vinegar is a robust and fruity vinegar made of cabernet grapes from the choicest vineyards in the Napa Valley. Before bottling the vinegar, the harvested grapes are fermented and aged in oak barrels to develop rich character and flavor, like that of a California wine. A luscious pairing with our selection of oils.

Mediterranean Tangerine Aromatic Oil. Sun-ripened fresh tangerines give this oil its distinct flavor. The aroma of this oil conjures the bright orange color of tangerine flesh. Drizzle with a splash of balsamic vinegar on roasted golden beets and arugula greens. Brush on grilled swordfish and serve with Bella's Olivada Olive Pesto.

Sicilian Lemon Aromatic Oil. The clean crisp flavor of whole lemons in first-pressed extra-virgin olive oil makes this finishing oil a versatile pantry essential. An elegant flavor enhancer, drizzle on soups or over grilled asparagus. Toss with oven roasted vegetables and a pinch of freshly chopped thyme.

The Essence of Eating Begins
with the Art of Food

OLIVE OIL SOAP

Bella Botanicals Olive Oil Soap is handmade on an organic farm near Atlanta, Georgia, exclusively for us. We have developed the fragrances and textures as a perfect extension of the Bella Cucina Artful Food product line. We use a high percentage of olive oil for the most emollient result. The essential oils used are of the highest quality and the organic herbs are grown on the farm. *Lemon Polenta, Oatmeal Espresso, Tangerine Orange, Peppermint Sage, Lavender and Rose Milk.*

PASTA SAUCES

Organic Passata al Pomodoro. Organically grown vine-ripened San Marzano tomatoes are picked at the peak of summer, peeled, and crushed for the most intense fresh tomato flavor. A leaf of fresh basil is added to scent every jar.

Farmhouse Sugo Pasta Sauce. A savory blend of our sweet sun-dried tomato, salt-packed anchovies, Italian capers, and fresh plum tomatoes. The result is a chunky farmhouse-style tomato sauce packed with flavor.

PEARL PASTA

From the wheat fields of the Mediterranean, this voluptuous pearl-like pasta (some call it couscous) will transform any meal into a flavorful eating experience. Treat it like an easy risotto, flavoring the liquid with stock or sautéed vegetables prior to cooking the pasta. Pearl pasta will soak up the liquid, taking on the rich qualities of the stock. Try these delicious varieties: *Mediterranean Pearl Pasta Mix with Porcini Mushroom and Sage; Mediterranean Pearl Pasta Mix with Sun-Dried Tomato and Basil; and Mediterranean Pearl Pasta mix with Corn and Cilantro.*

MARMELLATA

Lemon Pear Limoncello Marmellata. A surprisingly sweet combination of lemons, ripe pears, and the traditional Sicilian Limoncello liqueur make this a delicious condiment for artisan cheeses and Italian meats.

Preserved Orange Marmellata. Pure Sicilian oranges give this jam its vibrant color and flavor. Use as a breakfast topping, filling, or flavoring for dessert cakes.

Blood Orange Marmellata. Blood oranges are the prized fruit of Sicily. The distinctive red color of the citrus flesh occurs naturally, coloring the jam a bright crimson red. Produced seasonally at the height of the fruit's sweetness and available only during the winter months.

CRACKERS AND CONDIMENTS

Bella's Dipping Cracker is a savory cracker round with a slightly scalloped shape making it a perfect companion to our pestos and an easy appetizer with drinks.

Balsamic Mustard is a European-style coarse-ground mustard made with yellow and brown seeds, white wine, and pure balsamic vinegar for sweetness. Use Balsamic Mustard alone as a rich and tangy condiment for meats, or flavor your favorite marinade, vinaigrette, or sandwich spread.

Chestnut Honey Mustard. Inspired by our love of European varietal honeys, this smooth glaze-like mustard is flavored prominently with Italian chestnut honey, the rich honey taken from hives located in the chestnut tree forests of central Italy. Add garlic and orange juice to make a grilling glaze for salmon, pork, or chicken.

PRESERVED CITRUS

Preserved Lemons. An adaptation of Moroccan preserved lemons, we hand-pack whole lemons and Kalamata Olives in a salt brine, scented with fresh lemon leaves. Use the lemon rind to enhance stews, roasted chicken, fish, salads, or pasta dishes. A visually artful and colorful presentation.

Preserved Oranges. Perfectly sliced oranges are layered in canning jars with fresh California kumquats and simmered in a fragrant sugar syrup. Subtly flavored with orange flower water, Preserved Oranges are a versatile flavoring chopped over pork tenderloin before roasting. Chop fruit and macerate with fresh fruit juice and red wine for a new Sangria taste. Marinate shrimp or scallops with the fruit then grill or pan-sauté.

DOLCI

Dolci Cioccolati. Death by Chocolate Cookies. As sinfully rich as their name suggests, these cookies achieve that perfect balance of crunchy and chewy with their biscotti-like texture. Flavored with a hint of espresso, this double-chocolate walnut cookie can be enjoyed with cappuccino, or for a decadent treat, heat cookies in the microwave for 12 seconds and serve with vanilla bean ice cream.

Dolci Biscotti-Dried Cherry and Almond Biscotti. Hand-made, using the centuries-old artisan technique of baking the cookie twice for the perfect texture, our "bis-cotti" (Italian for twice-cooked) are crunchy to the tooth, but soft enough to enjoy without dunking. Enjoy Dolci Biscotti with freshly brewed espresso or a glass of Vin Santo. Serve as a dessert cookie with fresh fruit and lemon cream or crush biscotti for a tasty ricotta cheesecake crust.

Dolci Di Latte Milk Caramel Sauce. Cows grazing naturally in the Argentine countryside produce the sweetest milk for our Dolci Di Latte caramel sauce. Made in small batches in traditional copper cauldrons, the rich, balanced flavor of our caramel is exceptional. Heat and serve over ice cream or for a healthy snack, serve with fresh Fuji apple slices.

Dolci Nocciola Chocolate Hazelnut Sauce. Artisan chocolate spread flavored with a splash of espresso and freshly roasted hazelnut paste. Heat sauce and serve warm over cakes, cookies, or ice cream with chopped hazelnuts and mascarpone whipped cream.

DOLCI

Preserved Lemon Cream. A luscious, sweet dessert topping, our Preserved Lemon Cream is a lighter version of lemon curd. Using the whole egg instead of just the yolk creates its velvety consistency. For extra texture, we've added chopped bits of our Classic Preserved Lemon rind, introducing an occasional tart and frequent textural bite. Serve on scones for brunch or on fresh berries for an easy yet elegant dessert.

Cranberry Conserve. A sweet and tangy pantry essential, cranberry conserve is a year-round condiment for roasted pork, or grilled chicken and turkey sandwiches. It also makes a delicious dessert and breakfast topping. Serve with baked brie during the holidays, or top pancakes or waffles on the brunch buffet.

Croastata Sweet Butter Pastry Tarts. Made with sweet dairy butter, these individual serving pastry shells make a beautiful presentation on the dessert buffet. Fill with our Preserved Lemon Cream and fresh berries or with mascarpone cheese flavored with orange zest and topped with our Cranberry Conserve. ৩

INDICE
Index